FRAPPES AND FATALITIES

CUP OF JO BOOK 3

KELLY HASHWAY

To Ayla with love

CHAPTER ONE

Most people remember their first kiss, their first date, their first love. I remember my first sip of coffee. I was in third grade. My mom left her frappe on the counter and went to answer the door. I'd been eyeing it up since the second she made it. It was a thing of beauty with its whipped cream, crushed ice, milk, and cold espresso. It reminded me of a milkshake, something I loved at the time—truth be told, I still do. Yeah, I'm pretty sure my first love was coffee. And now, seeing the way the newly engaged couple is staring at each other at the engagement party Cup of Jo is catering, I see the same look in their eyes as I had that day when I was nine.

Camden Turner, my boyfriend and business partner, walks up beside me and places his hand on the small of my back. "I'd say our first catering gig is going extremely well. Everyone is loving the frappes and the flourless chocolate cake."

Cam is a baker, which makes him the perfect counterpart to my coffee-loving self. I can't really be blamed for the way I am. After all, my name is Joanna Coffee—as in Jo Coffee. I was literally born into the coffee business.

"Your cake is divine," I say. I was fortunate enough to sneak a piece for myself, though I could only eat one bite before I had to serve the frappes.

The happy couple is at the head table in the front of the dining room in the Reede Bed and Breakfast. The entire room is done up in pastel pink, not exactly my favorite, but I'm not the bride-to-be. Speaking of the bride-to-be, Jessica Scanlon is a twenty-five-year-old law school dropout. She works at the library now, shelving books. The rumor around town is she saw the movie *Legally Blonde* and thought she could be just like the main character and surprise everyone by being a great lawyer despite her appearance as a superficial blonde. Turns out, Jessica doesn't like law or school.

Her fiancé, Xander Pyle, is a lot more driven. He's an accountant, and from what I can tell, he adores Jessica. Good for them. They're only five years younger than I am, but that means we were never in school together, so I don't know them well at all. What I do know comes courtesy of the Bennett Falls rumor mill, which likes to hang out at my coffee shop and is headed up by my best customer, Mickey Baldwin.

The best man finishes his speech, which, thankfully, is

shorter than the maid of honor's. She droned on for about twenty minutes. Okay, it was twenty-one minutes and thirteen seconds. I timed it.

I feel bad for the guests who are finished with their cake and frappes and just waiting for the opportunity to get up from their tables.

"Excuse me," a woman at the table to my right says, holding a hand up in the air as if we're in school.

I walk over to her. "Yes?"

"We were wondering if we could get refills on our frappes. They're delicious, and that chocolate cake made us all really thirsty."

"Sure. I'll make six more right now."

"Oh, we only have five people at our table," she says.

I note the empty place setting. "Right. Give me a moment."

Cam follows me back into the kitchen just off the dining room. "Need help?"

"No, I can manage. We should be out of here soon." I get to work on the espresso.

"Tired?" Cam comes up behind me and massages my shoulders as I work.

"Yeah, it was a long day." Cup of Jo usually only stays open until five, but since we had this catering job, Cam and I have been on our feet since early this morning. I'm not used to working double shifts. "I'm starting to think I should have brought Jamar along tonight." Jamar is my one and only employee. I originally thought I'd have to hire another when Cam and I combined our businesses, but so far, it's been working out great with Jamar serving, Cam baking, and me making the drinks. I'm not opposed to the idea of hiring another employee, but I'm not going to rush into anything either.

"I'm looking forward to going home and crashing," Cam says.

I finish the espresso and immediately put it in the walk-in fridge to cool.

Elena Reede comes into the kitchen. "Oh good, you're both here. My serving staff was ready to clear the plates, but several tables are requesting more cake."

"I'll take care of that," Cam says. "I have more cakes in the fridge." He hurries off to grab them.

Elena follows him out. She's been running around all evening.

Once the espresso is cool enough, I blend some ice, milk, and a little sugar with the espresso. Then I pour the mixture into glasses and top them each off with some whipped cream.

"Jo," Elena says as she comes back into the kitchen. "Cam wants to know if you can grab another cake from the fridge."

"Sure, I'll bring it right out." I go to the fridge to grab two more cakes, just in case, and bring them to the dining room. By the time I get back to the kitchen, the frappes are no longer on the counter. I head to the dining room again to check the table that requested them. All five people have new drinks, so one of the wait staff must have served them for me. I can't help wondering why they couldn't get the cakes for Cam then. I shake off the thought, happy the night is winding down. I'm too tired to even think right now.

Thirty minutes later, Cam and I are loading up his SUV and heading home. He drops me off at my apartment complex.

"Want me to walk you up?" he asks.

"No. Go home. Get some rest." I lean over the middle console to give him a kiss goodnight.

"I can hang on to your coffee equipment until tomorrow if you'd like." He hitches a thumb over his shoulder to where my espresso machines and blenders are.

"Yes, please. They have to go back to Cup of Jo anyway."

"You got it." He gives me a smile before I step out of the car.

I wave before disappearing inside my apartment complex. The place used to be a resort, but after the tourism in the small town died down, it was converted into apartments. I take the elevator to the third floor. Midnight, the resident black cat, is sitting on my door mat, waiting for me. She meows when she sees me.

"Hungry?" I ask her.

Jamar pokes his head out of his apartment next to mine. "She's been waiting for you to come home. I tried to feed her, but apparently only you have the good tuna." He laughs.

Normally, I love hanging out with Jamar, but I'm so exhausted I'm hoping he doesn't follow me into my apartment. "She's picky about the brand."

"You look tired. Want to pass the tuna off to me and I'll feed her so you can get some rest?"

"You're the best, but I think I can manage to keep my eyes open long enough for her to eat. Then I'm totally crashing."

"See you tomorrow," Jamar says before slipping back inside his apartment.

"Come on," I tell Midnight as I open the door.

I go directly to the refrigerator and get her tuna. Once it's in the bowl I leave out for her in the kitchen, I take a quick shower and get ready for bed.

Through the window to the kitchen, I see Cam looks as tired as I do Sunday morning. My guess is he arrived at least an hour ago. I place my things under the counter and then go into the kitchen.

"Hey," he says, looking up at me.

"Hey, yourself." I scan all the baked goods on the cooling racks. "Were you unable to sleep or something?"

"I woke up at three. Don't ask why."

"Yikes. I'll go make you some strong coffee."

"Thanks." He gives me a small smile and then removes a tray of sticky buns from the oven.

I start up the coffee machines. After making frappes

all evening yesterday, I decide to make that today's special at Cup of Jo. They were a big hit at the party. I'm not sure how many I wound up making after all the refills. I get Cam his hot coffee first, though, sliding it through the kitchen window to him.

I make a ton of espresso ahead of time so I can let it properly cool. Then I wash out all the blenders again, even though I washed them last night before leaving the bed and breakfast. Once I'm finished, I prep the specials board, opting for bright neon green chalk.

As soon as I turn the sign on the door to read "Open," Samantha Shaw, my ex best friend and current fiancée of my former boyfriend, hurries inside.

"Jo, were you at the Reede B&B last night?" she asks.

"Yeah, we had a catering job. Why?" I walk back behind the counter. Samantha and I had it out last month when I finally confronted her about what an awful friend she was to me and let her know we currently aren't, nor will we ever again be, friends. Still, she comes in here every day, sometimes more than once, acting like nothing ever happened. That's Samantha for you. When we first met, I felt sorry for her. She was always getting picked on because she's so naïve. Now, I have trouble tolerating her complete lack of understanding of just about every situation.

"You haven't heard?" she asks me.

"Heard what?" I wish she'd hurry up and tell me whatever it is she wants to say so she can leave.

"Quentin got a call this morning."

7

Oh no. Whenever Detective Quentin Perry gets a call, someone was found dead. Was it Mary Ellen Reede? She's the owner of the Reede B&B, but at eighty-two years old, she isn't exactly up to running the place, so her daughter Elena takes care of that. Mary Ellen lives on the premises, though. She's a sweet woman.

Samantha is staring at me as if she's already clued me in and is waiting for my reaction.

"Samantha, what was the call about?"

"You really didn't hear?"

It's like talking to a small child. "No, I haven't heard anything. I've been asleep all night, and now I'm here, getting ready to start my work day."

"Oh, well, Quentin got a call from Elena Reede." She shakes her head like the news is too awful to say. "He didn't want me to hear the call. I could tell."

"But did you?" Does she even know what's going on?

She nods. "Murder."

"Someone was murdered at the B&B?"

"More like five someones."

Five people died? "What? How?"

She shrugs. "I don't know. They were found this morning. All dead in their rooms."

The door to Cup of Jo opens, and this time, it's Quentin who walks in. He marches right up to the counter.

"Shouldn't you be at the B&B investigating the murders?" I ask him.

"I am investigating the murders. Funny that you

know about them." His tone is accusatory, and the look in his eyes holds no friendliness at all. But considering the last time I spoke to him, I publicly humiliated him in front of a restaurant full of people, that seems about right.

"Your fiancée just told me about it."

Quentin's right arm whips out, and he pulls Samantha to his side as if protecting her from my words. "I have five dead bodies on my hands, Jo. Five. And do you know what they all have in common?"

I shouldn't goad him, but I can't help myself. "They attended the same engagement party? They all know the couple getting married? They all stayed at the Reede B&B?" I pause and meet his gaze. "Should I keep going?"

"They all drank your frappes."

I laugh, though it's actually not funny since he's accused me of poisoning people with my coffee before. "Everyone there did."

"They all had their glasses in their rooms with them."

What? They took them back to their rooms? That would mean they were the ones who asked for the refills. "It was the table of five."

"You should know."

"Me? I didn't even serve the drinks. Elena Reede had her own serving staff. Why would you suggest I should know what happened?"

"You tell me, Jo. Because from where I stand, you

made them those frappes, and right now every sign is pointing to those drinks being poisoned."

"You can't be serious. How many times do we have to go through this? You can't possibly think I poisoned those people."

"That's exactly what I think."

CHAPTER TWO

Cam comes rushing out of the kitchen. "What's going on?" His gaze volleys between Quentin and me.

"I'll need you both to come down to the station with me," Quentin says.

"Why Cam?" I ask. "He didn't make or serve the frappes." *I* didn't even serve them.

"You two work together and are dating. If you did something, I'm willing to bet my badge he knows about it." Quentin lets go of Samantha and gestures to the door. "Let's go."

Jamar isn't even here yet. I can't just leave. I grab my phone from my pocket and call him. "This is insane, just so you know," I tell Quentin before Jamar picks up.

"Hey, Boss. I'm on my way."

Our apartment complex is one mile from Cup of Jo, so Jamar will be here in a matter of minutes.

"Great. I need you to watch the place. How are you at making frappes? I already prepped the espresso."

"I'm fine now." Jamar's been learning to make all the drinks for times when I have to step out. I never thought I'd be leaving him alone for this reason, though. Not after the last time Quentin falsely accused me of poisoning someone. It's completely surreal.

I level Quentin with a look before telling Jamar, "I shouldn't be long. Hopefully, the Bennett Falls PD sees how insane this is and I'll be back in no time."

"I'm parking now. What's going on, though? Why is there a patrol car out front?"

"One guess," I say.

Jamar walks in and pockets his phone, so I pocket mine as well. "You're joking, right?" He walks right up to Quentin. "What are you accusing her of this time?"

"Murder," Samantha answers as casually as if she's placing a drink order.

"How many times are you going to do this?" Jamar asks. "Do you really enjoy making yourself look like a fool?"

"Jamar." I hold up a hand to stop him. I don't want Quentin to have any reason to bring him down to the station, too. "I'll handle this. You just take care of things here, okay?"

Cam removes his apron, the one with frilly white lace that used to belong to his grandmother. "There are scones in the oven. Take them out when the timer goes off. I've made enough baked goods to get you through the morning." He tosses the apron under the counter and takes my hand.

"I've got this," Jamar says. "Don't worry about a thing."

"Thanks, Jamar. We'll be back as soon as we can," I say.

Quentin kisses Samantha and motions for us to walk out first. "We'll take my car," he says.

No way am I sitting in the back of his patrol car like a criminal. "We're not under arrest, right?" I ask.

"Not yet, no." Quentin opens the driver's side door.

"Then we'll meet you at the station," I say, heading to Cam's SUV.

"Fine. I'll follow you." Quentin narrows his eyes. "No stops along the way." He gets in the driver's seat, and not a second too soon or I might have said something that would put me in the back of his patrol car for sure.

"I hate him so much," I tell Cam the second we're inside the SUV.

"Hate is not a strong enough word." Cam backs out of the parking space and drives to the station.

"Five people are dead. It has to be the only table of five. The one that requested the refills right before we stopped serving."

"That makes sense. Quentin is sure their deaths were due to poisoning?"

"Yeah. He said they all had their drinks in their rooms. I'm sure they're already testing them to find out exactly what poison was used."

KELLY HASHWAY

"But anyone could have poisoned the drinks after you made them."

"That's true. I left the kitchen to bring out two more cakes."

"We'll figure this out. Don't worry." Cam parks in front of the station, and Quentin pulls up right next to us as if he's afraid we'll make a run for it if he's more than ten feet away.

I swear the best thing that ever happened to me was him cheating on me. Otherwise, I might be Mrs. Quentin Perry right now. That thought is enough to give me nightmares.

He brings us to his desk instead of an interrogation room, so I'm thankful for that much. "Sit down. Both of you. And tell me exactly what happened last night."

I fill him in on how the table requested refills.

"Who requested them?" he asks. "I need specifics."

"I don't know her name. I don't think she's from Bennett Falls," I say.

"What did she look like?"

"She had red curly hair."

"That's Haley Roebuck. And you're right. She's not from Bennet Falls. She's from Highland Hills."

That's the next town over where my friend Lance's restaurant is.

"Then you made the drinks?"

I resist the urge to scream "Duh!" Instead, I just nod.

"And?" He waves his hand in the air, gesturing for me to continue.

"Elena Reede poked her head into the kitchen and asked me to bring out another cake from the walk-in cooler."

"Did you?"

"Yes. And I left the drinks behind. When I got back to the kitchen, they were gone."

"Gone?"

"Someone had brought them to the table that requested them."

"Who?" Quentin asks.

"I'm assuming one of the servers. I wasn't there to see it, though."

"Then anyone could have gone into the kitchen and poisoned the drinks," Cam says.

"Right. The kitchen was empty." I motion to Quentin's pad. "Aren't you going to write this down?"

Instead of answering, he asks, "Did you see anyone leave with their drink?"

"No, Cam and I went back to the kitchen to clean up. Then we left." I'm in complete disbelief that I'm in this position again. And so soon. "What poison did you find in the drinks?"

Quentin clears his throat. He hates sharing information with me. He claims it's because I'm not a cop, but really, I think he's afraid I'll solve yet another case before he does.

"Look, I can google this if need be. It was added to a drink but no one tasted it, so it's clearly tasteless. It also has to be water-soluble to be undetected by sight."

"Stop playing detective, Jo," Quentin snaps.

I narrow my eyes at him. "How can I when you clearly can't do your job?"

Cam reaches for my hand and squeezes it. "Calm down, Jo."

I force out a short laugh. "You'd think I would be used to this by now. That I could take it in stride since he keeps accusing me of poisoning people, but what I can't get past is how he's willing to pin every murder on me because he's pissed I made him look bad. Well news flash, Detective, you made yourself look bad. I'm not the one who cheated."

Quentin leans over his desk toward me. "Would you like me to arrest you? I could, you know."

"What evidence do you have? None?"

"The arsenic in the drinks you made."

Arsenic. At least, I know what poison was used now. "Like I said, I left the drinks unattended. Anyone could have added arsenic to them. I didn't even serve the drinks. So try talking to the wait staff. See who touched the drinks. See if anyone was spotted in the kitchen." Why do I always have to tell him how to do his job?

My phone rings.

"Don't even think about taking a call right now," Quentin says as I pull the phone from my purse.

Mo's picture is on the screen. Since my little sister happens to work in an office building directly across from Cup of Jo, and she comes in for her daily dose of caffeine every morning, I'm sure she's heard about me being dragged down to the station—that is if she didn't witness it from her office window, although I suspect she would have called me immediately if that were the case. I answer the call and hold the phone across the desk to Quentin. "Fine. You tell Mo how you made me come down here and are throwing out wild accusations yet again. I'll wait."

"Quentin, if you have my sister at the station again, so help me, I'll—"

I bring the phone to my ear before she can finish her threat. "Mo, I'm fine. Detective Perry can't solve yet another case, so he's blaming me. It's par for the course, really. I'll call you as soon as I leave here. Promise." I hang up before she can protest.

Quentin places both palms on the desk in front of him. "This isn't a joke, Jo. Do you think I like having to haul you in like this again?"

"Actually, I do think you enjoy blaming me. I just wish you'd realize once and for all, that I haven't done anything wrong. Stop being so quick to point your finger at me. Do your job, and find the guilty party. Now are we finished here?"

"You have nothing concrete to hold her," Cam says. "Jo didn't even know those people. You know she didn't do this."

"Get out of my sight. The both of you." Quentin waves his hand in the air, his face bright red.

"Gladly," I say, getting to my feet and storming out.

17

"What now?" Cam asks, starting the car and turning to look at me.

"We have to figure out who did this."

"You mean you want to investigate this case? Are you sure you want to get involved in another murder investigation?"

"What choice do I have? Quentin is content to blame me. If I don't figure out who did this, he'll shut down Cup of Jo again." I'm kind of surprised he hasn't already, but I guess since we catered the dessert and coffee at the bed and breakfast, Quentin assumes we used their equipment. And the fact that not everyone was poisoned means the poison was added to the drinks right before they were consumed. It wouldn't have come into contact with any of the equipment used to actually make the drinks.

"So, we're heading to the bed and breakfast?" Cam asks.

If Quentin goes there and finds us, he's going to be even angrier than he already is. But then again, if he doesn't see me investigating, he might be inclined to think it's because I'm guilty. Getting to lock me up for murder is about the only thing that would restore his reputation in this town, and I'm not about to let that happen.

I nod to Cam. "We go to the bed and breakfast."

CHAPTER THREE

I expect Elena Reede to be particularly unhappy when we walk into the bed and breakfast. I mean, this isn't the first time a murder investigation has led us here. But she looks almost relieved to see Cam and me.

She rushes over to us from the check-in desk. "Jo, Cam, I'm glad you're here. Detective Perry was quick to leave and speak to you both."

"Elena, do you know who served the frappe refills to the table of five when I left the kitchen to bring out more cakes?" I ask.

Elena nods and motions for us to follow her. She brings us to the kitchen, and I'm surprised it's not roped off with police tape. "Detective Perry is convinced someone poisoned the drinks and delivered them to that table. Since the kitchen was cleaned, they didn't find anything here. The dining room and the rooms where those five guests were staying are closed off, though."

"Why close the dining room but not the kitchen?" I ask. That doesn't make sense. What is Quentin thinking?

"I'm not sure. Closing the dining room shuts us down as far as serving meals, though, so in essence, it has the same effect."

I suppose that's true.

"He also told the staff to stay out of here," Elena says, and she gives me a small smile, as if it pleases her to defy Quentin's order.

Still, she looks too happy for someone whose place of business experienced five murders. And just like that, it clicks. She must think the murders will be what makes her mother finally concede to selling the place. It's no secret she hates working here. But would Elena go so far as to poison people and commit those murders herself to get rid of this place? After all, she is the one who asked me to get the cakes for Cam. Now that I think about it, she could have grabbed them herself. Why call me away from making and serving drinks? Was it so she could poison the drinks and deliver them to that table?

"Elena, did you see anyone in the kitchen after I left to deliver the cakes?" I ask, hoping to trick her into revealing more than she wants to if I'm correct about this.

"I'm not sure what you mean. When I asked you to get more cake, you were the only one in the kitchen."

It's possible she thinks I'm the guilty party but doesn't care since the murders might shut down the B&B for good.

"You didn't walk by or come into the kitchen yourself after I left to deliver the cakes?" I ask.

She shakes her head. "I went out to the front desk. A guest was having an issue with the safe in his room."

"Was the guest part of the engagement party?" Cam asks.

She nods. "Yes, he said he wanted to lock up some items for the night but couldn't get the safe to open."

Why would he try to take care of the matter during the engagement party? Why not wait until it was over and he was ready to lock up the items for the night? And why did he even need to lock something up when he'd be in the room all night with his valuables? None of it makes sense. Unless Elena is lying to us.

"If you'll wait here, I'll get the wait staff from last night so you can speak to them. I'm trying to keep all police investigation away from the guests. None of them is allowed to leave until the police finish talking to them, though, so my efforts might be futile."

"How is your mother handling all of this?" I ask.

"She doesn't know yet."

That surprises me. If Elena did commit the murders to get rid of the B&B, she'd be the first one to tell her mother about them.

"Her health has been declining. I don't want to upset her."

"I understand."

"Let me go get the wait staff for you." She walks away.

"What do you think?" Cam asks. "I can see the wheels turning in your head."

I bite my bottom lip as I consider what we know, which isn't much at all. "As happy as Elena is about all this, I don't think she had anything to do with the poisonings."

"Agreed. She would have told her mother and used it as an excuse to get rid of the place," Cam says, reiterating my thoughts.

"So that leaves the wait staff and the party guests."

"Right. Being that the kitchen was empty, it could have been any of them."

There were five tables of guests, each with six people, except for the one table of five. That makes twenty-nine people. Plus the couple at the head table. That's thirty-one people for the engagement party alone. It could take a long time to talk to all of them.

Elena returns with two women and one man. "Jo, Cam, this is Grace, Evan, and Teresa."

I recognize Grace after having met her during a previous case.

"If you'll excuse me, I have a few things to take care of. Detective Perry has been calling the guests down to the station a few at a time for questioning." Elena walks away.

I motion toward the entrance of the dining room. "Did any of you happen to serve frappes to the table over there?" I point to where the table of five was sitting last night.

"I did," Grace says.

This can't be that easy. "Did you get them from the kitchen?"

"No, I took them from this woman. She was trying to balance them on a tray, but she almost dropped the whole thing."

"Do you know who the woman was?" I ask.

Grace shakes her head. "One of the guests. She definitely didn't work here, or I'd know her."

"Could you describe her?" I ask.

"She had red hair."

Haley? The woman who asked me for the refills? "Was her hair curly?"

Grace nods.

I try to remember what Haley was wearing since she wasn't the only redhead at the party. "Was she wearing a coral top?"

"It was sort of orangey. Yes."

"Haley," I tell Cam.

"Thank you, Grace. Did either of you happen to go into the kitchen last night?" I ask Evan and Teresa.

"I cleared the cake plates at the end of the night," Evan says.

That was after the drinks were poisoned. "What about before that?"

"No, the place settings were already set up before the party started," Evan says.

And the cakes were brought to the tables by Cam and

me. Each table had their own cake. "Did you see anyone go into the kitchen besides Cam or me?"

Evan shakes his head, but Teresa's eyes widen.

"I did see someone. More than one person, actually. The bridal party was in the bathroom next to the kitchen. Then I think one or two of them slipped into the kitchen and came out holding a bottle of wine."

Cam turns to me. "Maybe they were planning an after party in one of the rooms."

"We'll need to talk to the bridal party then." I turn to the three servers. "Thank you. You've all been very helpful."

They nod and walk away, leaving Cam and me staring at each other, trying to make sense of what we heard.

"We know Haley was in the kitchen and so was the bridal party," I say. "But Haley was one of the victims, so it doesn't make sense that she would have poisoned the drinks."

"Right. Unless she wanted to commit suicide. She did request the refills," Cam says, "so it's not entirely out of the question."

No, it's not. "But since she's dead, that leaves us with questioning the bridal party."

"At least Quentin is questioning people down at the station. That means he'll be out of our way." Cam rubs one hand up and down my arm. "You okay?"

"Yeah, I—" I'm cut off by my ringing phone. I totally forgot to call Mo back. I pull the phone from my purse and see her face on the screen. "Sorry," I answer. "Cam and I are investigating, and I forgot to call you."

"What is going on? Is this about the murders at the B&B? I just read the article online. Five people are dead?"

I rehash what I know to get Mo up to speed.

"How dare people mess with perfectly good coffee? It's sinful."

I don't bother to point out that murder itself is a sin. "Cam and I are at the B&B. We just spoke to the wait staff. Now we're going to talk to some of the party guests."

"What can I do? I'm off today."

"I thought you told me you had to work today. Something about overtime." Mo was very animated and happy about the extra money when she mentioned it to me.

"My boss is a cheapskate and decided he didn't want to pay me. Don't get me started." Even though I can't see her, I'm sure she's waving her hand in the air in frustration. "But on the bright side, Wes took me to breakfast."

"Oh, and here I thought you were worried about me being at the police station, but really you were on a date."

"It's Quentin. The man is pathetic. I knew he wouldn't really arrest you. It would be too difficult for you to solve the case for him if you were behind bars. And besides, you were with Cam. He'd never let anyone lay a finger on you."

Cam smiles, having heard Mo.

"That's true. Back to your question, there's really nothing for you to do." As soon as the words leave my mouth, I realize I'm wrong. "Actually, now that I think about it, could you look into the five people who were poisoned? They aren't all from Bennett Falls, and I need to find out why they were targeted."

"Sure. Give me the names."

"Um, I don't have them all. I'll get them from Elena Reede and text them to you in a few minutes."

"Sounds good. Oh, and just so you know, Cup of Jo is packed. Mickey has a captive audience and is spouting theories on the murders."

"Of course, he is."

"Jamar is handling it just fine, though. Still, you really need to hire someone else if you and Cam are both going to leave Jamar like this."

"I know. I'll hire someone soon." Hopefully as soon as this case is over. "In the meantime…"

Mo groans. "You want me to bail him out, don't you?"

"Just offer a hand when he needs it. Please, Mo?"

"Fine. You owe me, though."

"Got it. Invite Wes."

"Maybe I will. I look cute in an apron."

"Thanks." I hang up. "We need to get the list of victims' names from Elena so Mo can look them up."

"She's going to do that *and* help Jamar serve customers?" Cam asks, following me to the check-in desk.

"She's Mo. She can handle it."

"You're probably right."

Elena is just getting off the phone when we approach the desk. "You should know that was Detective Perry. He asked if you two were here."

Just wonderful.

She smirks. "I told him if you were, I'm too busy to notice."

"Thanks, Elena. We appreciate it."

"Hey, if you ask me, you two will solve this long before he does."

"We could use your help with that. We need the names of the five victims."

"Oh, sure. I can do that. I suppose the media hasn't gotten a hold of the names yet."

"No, you know how it is. Until the police can notify next of kin, that info stays locked up tight."

Elena clicks a few keys on her computer and then jots down the names on a sticky note. "Here you go."

"Thank you." I quickly text Mo.

Just as I'm pocketing my phone, the engaged couple comes walking downstairs, looking anything but in love. I make a beeline right for them.

CHAPTER FOUR

"Excuse me," I say.

The woman looks at me. "Yes?"

"Hi, I'm Joanna Coffee, and this is Camden Turner. We catered your party last night." I realize it's probably not the best lead-in considering five of their friends were murdered with my frappes, but I don't want to start off on a lie.

"Why are you here? Shouldn't you be locked up?" The woman starts sobbing.

"I understand how upset you must be, but we're upset, too. Someone used our business to murder your friends. We want to find out who that person is just as much as you do." I try to keep my voice calm and soothing.

"Why should we believe you didn't do it?" the man asks.

"Can we sit down and talk, please?" I ask. "We'll explain everything."

The man shrugs, his hands in his pockets, and it dawns on me that he's doing nothing to console his future wife. Odd.

I motion for them to follow us to the living room. It's a big room, meant to accommodate a lot of guests. Of course, the engagement party brought in a lot more guests than the B&B is meant to accommodate. Several must have stayed in the same room with extra cots.

We sit down on the couch, though the man opts to sit in a chair.

"Can I ask your names?" I begin even though I already know their names. It just seems like a good place to start.

"Xander Pyle. That's Jessica Scanlon."

I'm assuming they've been fighting because the love I saw in their eyes last night is nowhere to be seen this morning. "Thank you. I know this is a particularly grim situation for the both of you. We don't want to take up too much of your time, but like I said, we're trying to find out who poisoned the drinks I made."

"Why should we believe it wasn't you?" Jessica asks.

"What reason would I have for wanting to kill any of your friends?" I ask. "And beyond that, why would I sabotage my own business?"

"She's right, Jess," Xander says. "It has to be one of the other party guests."

"You keep saying that, but they're our friends." She grips her hands together tightly in her lap.

At least, now we know why they've been fighting. She doesn't want to think anyone they know is capable of murder, and he's ready to throw one of their friends under the bus.

"What can you tell us about the victims?" I ask before they start yelling at each other.

"Donovan and Joseph are two of my groomsmen," Xander says. "I've known them for most of my life."

"What about their dates?" Cam asks. "Did you know them well, too?"

"Joseph was dating Haley for a few months. I didn't know Don's date, Lena. She seemed nice enough, though."

"Donovan Shepherd is a serial dater. We never met Lena before last night," Jess says, and I get the impression she's not crazy about Donovan.

"Okay, what about the fifth person at that table?" I ask.

Xander scoffs. "Drew Bloom. Feel free to look into him."

"Why would they look into Drew?" Jess asks. "He's dead, Xander. Give the poor man a break."

"You certainly did! He was in love with you, and you invited him to our wedding. He didn't even bring a date to the engagement party because he couldn't bear to be with anyone but you. You know he came here to try to stop the wedding. He probably poisoned the others and accidentally poisoned himself in the process." Xander is on his feet now.

"That's insane! Drew has never been anything but a perfect gentleman. How dare you, Xander?" She gets up and storms out of the room.

"See? She's always defending him." Xander's arm whips out in the direction Jess went. "I don't know why I agreed to let him come. I'm telling you he did this. The idiot just screwed up and killed himself, too. Or maybe he realized he wouldn't win Jess over in the end and decided to kill himself as well. Who knows? Are we done here?"

We can't force him to talk to us. It's not like we have badges. "Yeah, thank you for your time. I'm very sorry for your loss."

Cam dips his head at Xander as Xander walks out of the living room.

My phone rings. Mo again. "What's up, Mo?"

"Quentin is next door at Bouquets of Love."

Bouquets of Love is Samantha's flower shop, which happens to be located right next to Cup of Jo. While he goes to visit her a lot, I'm sure his presence now is also a way to check up on me. "We're on our way. Thanks for the heads-up."

"No problem. I like when you owe me."

I hang up. "We need to get to Cup of Jo right now. Quentin is at the flower shop."

Cam gets us to Cup of Jo in record time, but Quentin

is already inside. He crosses his arms and glares at us as we walk in.

I try not to look guilty as I walk right past Quentin and up to the counter, where I stash my purse. Mo moves to my side. "Thanks for covering for me while I ran to the store, Mo," I say loudly enough for Quentin to hear. I know no one else in here will rat me out. None of them likes Quentin.

"No problem. Did you two get the issue with that missing order cleared up?" Mo asks, playing right along.

"Yeah, it took longer than expected, but it's all fixed now," Cam says, joining us.

"It must have taken you a while," Quentin says. "Sam says she hasn't seen either of you all morning."

"Well, you're partially to blame for that, Detective. You did call us in to the station. By the time we got to the store after contacting our distributor, it was pretty crowded." I stare right into Quentin's eyes to let him know I'm not afraid of him.

"Then you didn't take a detour to the Reede B&B?" Quentin pushes.

"You obviously won't believe a word we say, so why don't you call Elena and ask her if we were there?" I ask, knowing he's already done just that and she covered for us.

Quentin lowers his arms to his sides. "Jo, I'm only going to tell you this once, so listen carefully. If I find out you're poking your nose into this investigation, I will charge you with murder."

I cock my head at him. "Are you planning to fabricate evidence, Detective? We both know that's the only way you'll be able to arrest me in connection with this crime."

"Don't make me get a search warrant."

"For what? You want to look around here? Or do you mean for my apartment?"

"Both."

I hold my arms straight out at my sides. "By all means, search. Be my guest. You won't find anything, and we both know it."

"Hey, Jo," Mickey says, walking up to the counter. "Can you make me another frappe? You know, just like the one you made me earlier." Since Quentin's back is to him and he can't see, Mickey winks at me.

Man, I love my little town. Any one of these people would provide me with an alibi to get Quentin off my back. "I'd be happy to, Mickey." I smile before turning my back to make the drink.

By the time I'm finished, Quentin is gone. "Thank you, Mickey. You didn't have to do that. I don't want you lying to the police for me."

"Who lied? You've made me frappes before. If you ask me, that counts as *earlier*. I didn't lie at all."

I grab a chocolate stick and place it in the frappe. "On the house," I tell Mickey.

He dips his head in thanks before returning to his table. I'm sure he'll tell the people gathered around him how he outsmarted Detective Perry.

"We'd better lay low," Cam says, motioning to the

patrol car still parked outside. "I have a feeling he'll stick close by to make sure we don't leave."

"This is why the man can't solve cases. He's too busy watching me all the time."

At five o'clock, Cam, Jamar, Mo, and I all head to my place for dinner. I whip up a quick stir-fry with mushrooms, red pepper, and onion. Then I fry up some breaded pork cutlets I prepped the day before. I toss it together in some spicy Szechuan sauce, and in about fifteen minutes, we're seated at my kitchen table.

"This is so spicy but so good," Mo says before taking a large sip of her margarita, courtesy of the pitcher Jamar made for us.

"You know I love spicy foods," I say. Quentin hates spicy food, so maybe that's why I'm craving it this evening.

"How do you plan to solve this case with Quentin looking over your shoulder?" Jamar asks.

"He can't watch me all the time. He has to question the engagement party guests."

"Speaking of the guests, how did they fit so many people at the B&B?" Mo asks.

"Easy, after Sherman Cromwell died, his longstanding room was rented out again. And Elena is staying in her mother's room. That gave them two more rooms to book. With everyone doubled up or in some cases quadrupled up with double beds in the room, they all fit."

"You know what doesn't fit?" Mo asks.

"What?" I turn to face her as I pop a mushroom into my mouth.

"Donovan Shepherd and Joseph Dunbar went to college together. They were roommates."

"Why is that odd?" Jamar asks.

"It's not. They both grew up with Xander Pyle. Their social media sites link the three. Tons of photos, a lot of history there. But then there's Drew Bloom. He doesn't fit at all. He's not on any of their social media sites. Not a one. So why was he seated with them?"

"I have a theory about that." I take a sip of my drink before continuing. "Xander hated Drew because Drew was in love with Jess."

Mo whips out her phone. "What's Jess's last name?"

"Scanlon," I say, remembering because she's the one I spoke to on the phone when she hired us to cater the party.

"Bingo! They're linked. She's all over Drew's photos, too."

I nod. "And Xander hated that. My guess is that the two groomsmen were supposed to keep an eye on Drew and most likely keep him away from Jess."

"That makes sense," Cam says.

"Okay, but if that's the case, who would kill them all? And what about the women at the table?"

"Xander and Jess didn't know Lena, but apparently

Joseph had been dating Haley for a little while," I say, considering it for a moment. "This probably isn't about the women."

"Unless there's something we don't know," Cam says.

Right now, there's a lot we don't know. "You're right. It's too soon to rule anything out."

"Then what's the next step?" Jamar asks.

"According to the wait staff we spoke with, the bridal party was in the kitchen. And Haley came out with the drinks shortly after that. She must have gone into the kitchen to see why the drinks were taking so long." I put down my fork. "She might have seen me leave to help with the cakes and thought I forgot about the drinks."

"So she went into the kitchen to see for herself," Mo says.

"Maybe. But in the time after I left, someone poisoned the drinks, and we know for certain that the wedding party had the opportunity to do so."

"But did someone in the wedding party also have the motive?" Cam asks.

"That's what we're going to find out."

CHAPTER FIVE

Cam and I are careful to stick around Cup of Jo until both Samantha and Quentin get their morning caffeine fixes. We need to be seen at work like any other day so Quentin doesn't figure out what we're doing. Mo even left her car keys with me so we can take her car and leave ours parked out front to make it look like we're still at work.

Samantha and Quentin linger near the table Mickey usually sits at, but Mickey isn't even here yet. He's a nighttime custodian at the local high school, which means he spends his mornings, which I suppose are evenings for him since they're after his work shift, here. I guess being here late yesterday threw off his sleep schedule.

Samantha comes back up to the counter. "Can I get a double chocolate chip muffin warmed up and another cup of mocha coffee?"

"Sure." I ring her up and then go to the window to ask Cam to warm up one of the double chocolate chip muffins. As quickly as possible, I pour a large mocha coffee and cap it, hoping she takes the hint that the order is to-go.

Once her muffin is warmed, I place it in a to-go box. "Here you go. Have a nice day."

"Aw, thanks, Jo. You, too." She smiles widely, completely oblivious, as usual, that I'm giving her the brush-off.

Quentin glares at me as he holds the door open for Samantha. Just to annoy him, I smile and wave.

"If it were me, I would have waved with one finger," Mrs. Marlow says, making me laugh. She's probably in her seventies, but don't tell her that because she acts like she's in her thirties.

"I'll try to remember that for next time," I say.

"Oh no, dear, you're much too good for that. I'll do it for you next time. I'd like to see him try to put handcuffs on me."

I love her spunk. "What can I get for you?"

"Well, I was hoping for that young man's phone number." She gestures to Jamar, wiping down a table in the corner. "But I'll settle for some coffee and a nice piece of crumb cake."

"You got it, and I'll put in a good word for you with Jamar. I happen to know he's single." I wink at her.

"Don't waste your time. I'm afraid he couldn't handle me." She winks back.

"You're right. He probably couldn't." I pat her hand before going to get her order.

I really do love my regulars. I've known most of them since I was in diapers, and some of them like to remind me of that fact.

About an hour later, the coast seems clear. Quentin's patrol car is gone. All that's left is for Cam and I to sneak out and across the street to Mo's car. I signal Jamar, who gives a discreet nod before casually walking up to the counter to start taking orders. I'm pretty sure he's enjoying being stealthy.

Next, I tap my hand in the window to the kitchen to signal Cam. He removes his apron and stores it on the shelf under the big island in the middle of the kitchen. Then he walks out and meets me by the far door, the one that used to belong to Cam's Kitchen before we knocked down the wall between our two places. We exit and head right to avoid walking by Bouquets of Love. We go to the traffic light and cross at the crosswalk. Mo parked farther down than usual, but if Sam is looking out the window, she'd still see us get into the car. We have to hope she doesn't have her nose pressed to the glass at the moment.

We get in the car as quickly as possible, and I start the engine. As soon as it's clear, I back up and drive down the street in the opposite direction of Sam's flower shop. As far as I can tell, we made it without being seen. The only question is would Quentin go to the bed and breakfast today in hopes of catching us there?

I decide to call ahead to Elena Reede and find out.

Cam dials since my phone isn't hooked up to the Bluetooth in Mo's car. He puts the call on speaker and holds it up for me so I can keep both hands on the steering wheel.

"Reede B&B. This is Elena speaking. How can I help you?"

"Elena, it's Jo Coffee."

"Yes," she says, and her tone implies she doesn't want to say my name, which can only mean one thing.

"Is Detective Perry there right now?"

"Yes, that's correct."

Great. Now what?

"I need to speak with the bridal party. Is there any way you can convince them to meet Cam and me at the park?" Quentin wouldn't be caught dead in the park. He hates birds, and there are plenty scavenging for food there.

"I'm booked solid at the moment, but let me see what I can do. Can I put you on a brief hold?"

"Sure," I say, realizing she must want to get rid of Quentin before she finishes talking to me.

"She's pretty good at this," Cam says.

"Everyone in this town seems to be. It's a little disconcerting when you think about it."

"Are you imagining a crime pulled off and covered up by the entire population of Bennett Falls?" he asks me with a smirk.

"Now I am! How terrifying is that thought?" I shiver.

But then again, that crime might involve getting rid of Detective Perry. Hmm. No, I can't think like that.

"I'm back," Elena says. "Yes, that will work. You said you wanted to check in early, around ten thirty. Is that correct?"

"Yes, we'll meet them at ten thirty," I say, realizing what she's really telling me.

"Very good then. I'll go ahead and book that reservation for you."

"Thank you, Elena."

Cam ends the call, and I turn toward the park.

"Is the plan to find out who was in the kitchen and what they did while they were in there?" he asks me once we're parked.

"Yes, but more importantly, we need to find a motive. Why would someone set out to murder five people, especially when only two of those five are truly linked by more than a few months?"

"What if the intended target was only one person at that table?" Cam asks.

"You think someone poisoned all five drinks to make sure the person the poison was intended for died no matter which drink they were served?" I open my car door and step out. It's not a bad theory.

"It's possible."

"But then who is the most likely target?" I meet Cam's eyes, and we both say, "Drew."

"That would make Xander look guilty," Cam says.

"Agreed. But I don't think Xander would kill two of his really good friends since childhood."

"Who else would want Drew dead, though?"

We walk to a set of benches in the middle of the park, just off to the right of the playground area where a mother and her young son are playing on the swings.

"What if Jess did it?" I ask. "Maybe she was sticking up for Drew when we talked to her in order to throw us off. It's possible she was annoyed he'd shown up without a date and decided she needed to get rid of him before he did something to wreck her upcoming nuptials."

"But then why fight with Xander about it? If she was trying to save her marriage, I don't think she'd pick a fight with her fiancé like that."

He's right. I'm missing something. Something big.

A car pulls up, and five women step out. Given the way they're all looking around as if lost, I know this is the bridal party. I stand up and wave them over to us.

The woman in front has jet-black hair to her waist. "What's this about? We just spoke to the police at the B&B."

"You spoke with Detective Perry? Does he know you were all coming here to talk to us?"

"No." The woman crosses her arms. "We were told there was an excursion booked for us. We thought it was a spa day or something, yet here we are in the middle of a park."

"Relax, Justine. Let's just figure out what they want." A blonde woman with a pixie cut steps up to us. "I'm

April. We just got a call from the lady at the bed and breakfast telling us why we're really here. Not everyone is thrilled, as you can clearly see."

"I'm sorry about that. The detective on the case isn't exactly thrilled to have help, hence the secrecy, but we want to find out what happened to your friends."

"They weren't our friends," says a woman with glasses.

"Laura, that's awful to say," April reprimands her.

"It's the truth, though. We barely know Xander's friends. Their dates were total strangers to us, and then there's Drew."

"What can you tell us about Drew?" I ask. "We heard he was in love with Jessica."

"You can say that again," says a brunette who hasn't spoken yet. "I'm Nina. I'm the maid of honor. Drew showed up without a date, and Jessica pretty much lost it."

"Nina," says the remaining blonde woman.

"Paige, you know it's true. Jess went berserk." Nina turns back to us. "Jess was always nice to Drew. I'm not sure why because the guy is a major tool. He was always following her around, and maybe she liked the attention. I don't know. I think she might have invited him to the engagement party to get it through his head that she was taken, you know? But he showed up alone and asked to speak to Jess in private."

"When was that?" I ask.

"Right before the party."

"Yeah, that's right," Paige says, bobbing her head.

"It's the first time I've seen Jess get upset with Drew," Nina says. "Her plan backfired. Instead of understanding he had no shot with her, Drew declared his love for her and asked her to call off the engagement."

April gasps. "I didn't know he did that. Why didn't you tell us?"

"Because Jess asked me not to tell anyone. She didn't want Xander to find out. She planned on uninviting Drew to the wedding. She figured that would end it."

Justine swats her hand in the air. "Why are there so many birds? It's not even that warm yet."

"They're nowhere near you. Stop swatting. You look deranged," Paige says.

"Were you guys planning an afterparty in one of the rooms?" I ask.

Nina nods. "Yeah, Jess got a bottle of wine from the kitchen."

"Was anyone else in the kitchen when you grabbed the wine?"

Paige shakes her head. "No. Jess saw you leave and figured we could sneak in and grab the wine. We tried to grab two bottles, but then someone else came in the kitchen."

"Who?" Cam asks.

"Joseph's date. What was her name?" April asks the other girls, who just shrug in response.

"Haley," I say.

"Yeah, her." April nods.

"What did she do in the kitchen?" Cam asks.

Laura pushes her glasses up on the bridge of her nose. "She took some drinks and put them on a tray."

"Can we go now? I really need a mani-pedi," Justine says, holding up her right hand and inspecting her nails. "My cuticles are a disaster."

"Yeah. Enjoy. Thank you for taking the time to talk to us," I say.

"There's a nail salon one street over," Cam says. "Just walk around that building. It's on the right side."

"Thanks." Nina winks at Cam before leading the group in the direction of the salon.

"Did she wink at you?" I ask him.

He laughs. "I think she did. Apparently, she didn't hear that I'm already taken." He slips one arm around my waist and places a kiss on the side of my head.

"Well, I think we only learned a few important things from that conversation."

"No one liked Drew, so if one person at that table was the intended target, it's most likely him," Cam says.

"Yes. And whoever messed with the drinks must have done it right before the bridal party went into the kitchen."

"How didn't you or they see them, then?" Cam asks.

"I don't know, but I'm convinced when we find out who was in the kitchen at that time, we'll know who the killer is."

CHAPTER SIX

"Jo, you missed the best impression of Quentin today," Mo says at dinner. We decided to go to S.C. Tunney's to support our friend Lance's restaurant.

"Who was doing impressions of Quentin?" I ask.

"Mrs. Marlow," Jamar says. "She did one of you, too, actually."

"Of me?" I take a sip of my water.

"Yup. First, she pretended to be Quentin saying he was watching you and don't make him take you out of Cup of Jo in handcuffs." Jamar starts laughing. "Then she turned around and imitated you, saying, 'Don't let the door hit you on the way out,' and she waved one finger in the air at him."

"The bad part was that Sam saw the whole thing," Mo says.

Oh no. She won't know better than to tell Quentin what happened, and he is not going to handle it well.

"Who cares?" Jamar says, bobbing one shoulder. "Besides, he might not even think she's retelling the story correctly. You know how she is."

"Is he making any progress with the case?" Mo asks me.

I place my linen napkin on my lap. "I don't know. He's not keeping me in the loop. After I embarrassed him in here last month, he's not being very friendly."

"That man is so up and down. I mean he was nice to you right after you told him off. Now he's holding a grudge again." Mo scoffs.

"I think he can't handle knowing Jo is better at his job than he is," Jamar says. "It's not good for his ego. Plus, everyone in town has been particularly nasty to him ever since."

"Yeah, that's not helping my situation. As much as I love how everyone is supporting me, it's going too far."

"I can spread the word that that's the case," Jamar says. "Consider it done tomorrow."

All he'll need to do is let Mickey know, and everyone will back off Quentin. Hopefully, that will help.

"Hey, guys," Lance says, walking over to the table in his chef's attire.

"Hey, Lance. We all just ordered the special," I say.

"Oh, good. You're going to love it. No seafood allergies here, right?" he asks, looking around the table at everyone. After a previous case involving fish allergies, Lance is being extra careful.

"We're all good," I tell him.

"Great. So, Jo, I wanted to tell you that the couple in town for their engagement party, the one you catered, ate here Friday night."

"Really?"

Lance squats down next to me at the table. "Yeah. They were all loving and really sweet together. But then a group of people came in that they clearly knew, and the mood changed in an instant."

Sounds like Jess and Xander. Their feelings for each other change on a dime. "Do you know who those people were?" I ask.

"All I know is it was a table of five. Three men and two women."

"Seriously?"

He nods. "I know. When I heard five people were poisoned, I couldn't help thinking it was the same five people."

"What makes you say that?" Cam asks.

"Well, the one guy was glaring at the couple. From the looks of it, he was the only one without a date."

"That must have been Drew Bloom."

"How did you know he was the one without a date?" Mo asks.

"Well, at first, it was hard to tell. Two of the men weren't acting like they had dates, so I thought maybe the two men and the second woman were all just friends. But the one guy didn't talk to any of the others, so I figured he was the fifth wheel."

Donovan and Lena had just started dating, so they

wouldn't really look like a couple. That makes sense. But why would Drew even go out with the others? Unless he knew Jess was going to be at the same restaurant.

"I don't know if that's helpful in any way, but I wanted to let you know," Lance says. "I don't plan on talking to your ex about it."

"I don't blame you, Lance." The last time Quentin talked to Lance, Lance was throwing him out of the restaurant, and the time before that, Quentin was trying to pin a murder on Lance. The two don't have the best history.

Lance stands up. "Well, I have to get back to the kitchen. If you need anything, let me know."

"Thanks, Lance."

"I think Cam's theory that there was only one real target is spot-on," Mo says. "It has to be Drew."

"You think Xander or one of the groomsmen is the killer?" I ask her.

"Why not? It's really the only thing that makes sense."

"Hey, sorry I'm late," Wes says, hurrying over to sit next to Mo. Mo and Wes have been pretty much inseparable since they met at work. You'd never guess they haven't been dating all that long. "What did I miss?"

I like Wes, but I don't exactly want to drag him into this murder investigation. If I scare him off by constantly being wrapped up in crimes, Mo will never forgive me. "Nothing at all," I say.

Since Quentin spent all of Monday interviewing the party guests at the bed and breakfast, I don't anticipate he'll show up there today. So once again, Cam and I work at Cup of Jo in the morning just long enough to make our presence known before slipping away.

Mrs. Marlow comes up to the counter with a big smile on her face. "He won't be coming in here today, Jo. Don't you worry."

"I heard about your performance yesterday. Apparently, you have a talent for impersonating police detectives and certain coffee shop owners."

"Not to toot my own horn, but I did get a standing ovation." She smiles, clearly pleased with herself.

"I also heard Samantha was in here at the time."

"Now don't go thinking you'll make me feel sorry for her. She's just as much a cheater as Quentin is. She knew what she was doing."

I'm not sure she really understood what she was doing at the time. "Still, I'm trying to be the bigger person."

"You are, sugar. You are." Mrs. Marlow pats my hand. "Now, can I place my order, or do you want to reprimand me some more?" She winks.

"What can I get you?"

"I'll take a cheese Danish and a large dark roast with extra cream and sugar."

"Coming right up." I pour the coffee first.

Cam comes out of the kitchen. "Almost ready to go?"

"Yeah, can you grab a cheese Danish for Mrs. Marlow for me?"

"Of course. Are you dining in, Mrs. Marlow?" he asks her.

"Naturally. I need to get my morning gossip from Mickey to start my day."

I hand her the coffee and ring her up. She's eyeing up the chocolate sticks in the jar by the register, so I slip one out and hand it to her. "On the house."

"Thank you, dear."

"You're welcome. No more impressions today, though, okay?"

"Okay, Mom." She rolls her eyes at me and then smiles to show she's only kidding.

I turn to Cam and tug on the edge of his frilly apron. "You're not going in this, are you?"

"What? I thought it might deter the maid of honor, Nina."

"Why don't you just try holding my hand if she comes around?" I suggest.

He smiles at me as he removes the apron and places it under the counter.

"Jamar, are you good?" I ask him.

"Yeah, but, Jo, you are planning to hire someone else soon, right?"

"Tell you what. I'll text Mo and ask her to print out a general job application for me. We'll put them up at the register."

51

"Or I can ask my friend Robin. She worked at the gym with me, and she's looking to get out of there now that they changed managers. The new guy hits on her all the time, and she can't stand it."

"You'll vouch for her?"

Jamar bobs his head. "Oh, yeah. She's a great worker. Always on time. Never complains. Great personality."

"Tell her she's got the job. Invite her over today if you'd like." I turn to see Cam staring at me. "Oh no." I clamp my hand over my mouth. "I'm so sorry. I can't believe I just did that without consulting you."

He laughs. "It's okay, Jo. You need help out here. My domain is the kitchen. Now if you hire someone to bake without consulting me, I'd be upset. But this is to make and serve your coffee."

"But she'll be serving your baked goods as well. I never should have done that. I'm so sorry, Cam." I grab the front of his shirt in my hands.

He leans down and presses a kiss to my lips. "Jo Coffee, you do not need to run every decision by me. Besides, Cup of Jo is your baby. You run it. I'll take care of the kitchen. That's the way I like it. If I'm being honest, I don't want to deal with the business end of it all. I just want to bake. That's what I love."

"You really are amazing."

"I know." He laughs and wraps an arm around me. "Now, it's time to act like spies and slip out of here undetected."

"Right. Let's go."

We make it to the bed and breakfast, and thankfully, there are no patrol cars out front. Elena is at the check-in desk even though the current guests can't leave town, which means no new guests can arrive since the place is booked to maximum capacity.

"Jo," Elena says, walking over to greet us. "The police have searched every room. They haven't found any traces of arsenic anywhere. They really don't have any suspects either. They're at a complete loss. Please tell me you have something."

"Actually, we don't. I'm sorry. We were hoping to talk to the groomsmen, though."

"Oh." Her face falls. "You know, as much as I want to sell this place, this isn't how I want things to go. I don't want my mother's dream to end because of an unsolved murder."

"I know. We're doing everything we can. I promise. If we don't find the killer soon, the police are going to circle back to suspecting me." If they ever really stopped.

She nods. "I can't imagine this is good for you either. I'll call up to the groomsmen. Do you want to use the living room again?"

"Please."

"Go on in. I'll send them there." She picks up the phone on her desk to make the calls.

Cam and I walk into the living room and sit down on the couch. Cam seems lost in thought, so I ask, "What are you thinking?"

"You know, the bathrooms are right next to the

53

kitchen, which means anyone could have snuck out of the bathroom and into the kitchen without being seen."

"If only this were high school and people had to sign out to use the restroom," I say. "We could ask if anyone used the bathroom at that time, but they could easily lie about it."

At the sound of footsteps, I raise my head to see three men walk into the living room. "Thank you for meeting with us. Please, have a seat," I say.

"Are you with the police?" the tallest of the men asks.

"I've been known to assist the police with certain cases," I say, which isn't a lie, even if I am skirting around the truth about this particular case.

He nods. "I'm Owen Pierce, the best man. This is Chris Lang and Adam Kane."

"How well did you three know Drew Bloom?" I ask.

They exchange a tense look, but no one answers.

"I see. We're aware that Mr. Bloom was pining after Jessica. It seems like everyone here didn't want Drew to be part of the wedding festivities."

"That's putting it mildly," Owen says.

"Did anyone dislike him enough to want to harm him?" I ask.

Chris laughs. "You aren't seriously asking if one of us tried to kill Drew."

"Someone at that party killed five people," I say. There's no "tried" about it.

Adam narrows his eyes at me. "Weren't you the one who served those drinks?"

"Actually, no. I made them, yes, but I didn't serve them. The drinks were left unattended in an empty kitchen, where anyone from the party could have poisoned them. We know the bridal party was in the kitchen. The question is, were any of you as well?" My gaze volleys back and forth between them.

"I was," Owen says. "I didn't poison the drinks, though. I followed Haley in there."

"Why?" I ask.

"The only reason Joseph knows Haley is because of me. I dated her first. He went behind my back and dated her after we broke things off."

"Why was it a problem for him to date your ex?" Cam asks.

"Seriously man? You don't date a friend's ex."

"Did you still have feelings for Haley?" I ask.

"That's beside the point."

"Not really. Did you still care enough about her to want Joseph out of the picture?"

"You think I poisoned Haley?" He scoffs. "I wanted her back. I didn't want her dead." Owen stands up. "I'm done here. I don't have to tell you anything." He walks off without another word.

"Let me give you a tip," Adam says. "It wasn't one of us. Sure, we all hated Drew for Xander's sake, but none of us would commit murder for him."

"What about Xander?" I ask. "Do you think he'd commit murder to keep Drew away from Jess?"

Chris shrugs. "Maybe, but he'd never kill Don and Joseph in the process. That part doesn't make any sense."

"I'm telling you there's no way someone in the wedding party did this," Adam says.

"When is the wedding?" I ask. "I mean this was an engagement party, yet the wedding party is already established? That has to mean the ceremony is close."

"Two months away. Jess wanted a June wedding. They got engaged four months ago, but Jess didn't want to have the party until spring."

I'm sensing Jess likes to get her way. "Thank you for your time."

"We aren't getting anywhere on this case, are we?" Cam asks once they leave.

"Unfortunately, no. No one seems to have a good enough reason to commit murder, but this was clearly premeditated. Someone came here with poison, and that same person slipped that poison into five drinks." But why?

The sound of voices draws my attention to the library. I stand up and press a finger to my lips to let Cam know I want to hear what's being said. As we get closer, I recognize the voices. It's Xander and Nina, the maid of honor.

"She's being completely unreasonable. I just lost two of my closest friends. I really don't care about bridesmaid dresses right now."

"I know, Xander. I'll talk to her. We'll fix this. Trust me."

"Their families should be here tomorrow. I have to worry about that. And the services after that. I don't want to hear about wedding preparations until all of this is over."

"I'll take care of it. You go do whatever you need to, and if there's anything I can do, let me know. I'm here for both Jess and you."

"Thanks, Nina. I know I can always count on you."

I turn back to Cam. "He sounds pretty upset."

"Yeah, but it's still possible that he intended to kill Drew and accidentally killed his two friends as well. That pain in his voice could be guilt."

CHAPTER SEVEN

Jessica comes down the stairs, screaming. "What's next? We all have to take polygraph tests, and they flat-out ask us if we poisoned those people?"

Why is she so angry? Cam and I move toward the front entrance to see what's going on.

"Jess, they're talking to everyone. It's their job," April says.

"Personally, I'm all for the polygraph test," Paige says. "It would clear my name so I can leave this place. There's a reason I moved away from this town when I turned eighteen. I didn't want to come back, and now I'm stuck here."

"Poor you," Jessica says. "It's not *your* wedding that's getting ruined."

"And you're not the one who died," Paige says. "Man, Jess, you're being really insensitive right now."

"Whoa!" Nina rushes into the room. "Okay,

everyone. Emotions are on high. Let's all take a step back and calm down."

Personally, I think letting them turn on each other might draw out the killer, but I guess Nina is only trying to be a good maid of honor by attempting to restore order.

"They're making me go back to the station," Jess says. "Will you come with me, Nina?"

"Of course, I will."

Xander finally enters the hallway, but Nina holds up a hand and mouths, "I've got it." Then she leads Jessica outside.

"You two are back?" Xander asks Cam and me.

"Yeah, we were just talking to your groomsmen."

"You want my opinion? Drew did this. He poisoned himself and my friends because he knew he couldn't have Jess. You know, like a murder-suicide kind of thing."

"How well did you know Drew?" I ask.

"Not well at all, but one encounter and you knew the guy was unhinged. I don't know why Jess put up with him."

I think I do. I think Jess liked the attention. He made her feel special. But then it got to be too much, and she lashed out at him. Maybe that was enough to make him snap. But then how would he have gotten the arsenic? It's not exactly something people carry around with them when they travel. And poisoning isn't usually a crime of passion. It distances the killer and victim too much.

I really hate that I know that. I blame Quentin for

always talking to me about his cases. He got me started on all this, and now it's like I'm addicted to solving murders. I can't rest until I know how and why they were committed. In this case, I know how, but the why is still as fuzzy as it was from the start.

Xander walks away, apparently done with us. As I watch him walk upstairs, I realize what I need to do next.

"Elena?" I ask as I approach her desk again. "Are the rooms still crime scenes?"

"The police have already searched the rooms from top to bottom. Detective Perry told me not to let anyone in there, though."

"Oh. I was hoping to see them."

Elena looks around. "I won't tell if you won't." She clearly wants this case over as much as I do if she's willing to openly defy Quentin's orders. I'm not about to stop her. She grabs two room keys from behind the desk and motions for us to follow her upstairs.

At the top of the stairs, we turn left. She brings us to a room in the middle of the hallway. "This is where the two couples were staying," she says as she opens the door.

There are two queen-size beds in the room, both made. I doubt Quentin let Elena's staff make the beds, so this strikes me as odd.

"They must have died before getting into bed," I say.

Elena nods. "That's what Detective Perry told the coroner when they were here."

"Is that what led them to thinking the deaths were the result of poisoning?" I ask.

Elena nods again. "Detective Perry found the drink glasses next to the bodies. Since no one had gotten changed out of their party clothes or gotten into bed for the night, he assumed they'd been poisoned. So they took the glasses to test the contents of the drinks."

That's a logical conclusion to make. At least Quentin didn't jump to accusing me just to make me suffer. And if I'm being honest, he hasn't really pressed to pin this crime on me since the very beginning. He's either avoiding me because the town is taking my side in our breakup, or he really doesn't think I had anything to do with this.

"Where were the bodies found?" I ask Elena.

She moves toward the dresser. "Um, one of the men was found on the floor in front of the dresser. And I think his date was at the foot of the bed."

"And the other couple?" Cam asks, looking around, I'm assuming for signs of anything that was disturbed when they died.

"The one man was in the doorway to the bathroom. I'm not sure about the other woman. Sorry."

"No need to apologize. This is very helpful, Elena. Thank you." I move to a stain on the carpet near the bathroom. I don't know if it was Joseph or Donovan, but he must have been carrying his drink and dropped it here. This is the fourth time one of my drinks was connected to a crime scene. You'd think I'd be used to it by now, but it's still disconcerting.

"Where are their things? Suitcases and such?" I ask Elena.

"The police took them. They wanted to search their belongings to check for traces of poison on them."

"Do they really think one of the deceased people was responsible for the poisoning?" Cam asks, rubbing the back of his neck. "That just doesn't seem likely at all to me."

"To be honest, I suspect Detective Perry doesn't know what to think," Elena says. She fidgets with her fingers. "Jo, I'm worried he's going to question me next. I was in the kitchen. You saw me."

"You only poked your head into the kitchen long enough to tell me Cam needed more cakes," I say. "You left right after that."

She looks down at the carpeting. "I did go back into the kitchen while you were gone."

"You did? Why?" I ask.

"The bride wanted a bucket of ice for her room. I guess they brought wine or something they wanted to chill."

No, it was for the wine the bridal party planned to steal from the kitchen. They must have asked Elena for the ice, and while she was delivering it to the room, they snuck into the kitchen and stole the wine.

"So you just got some ice from the freezer?" I ask.

"Yes. I swear. I grabbed the bucket, filled it with ice, and left."

"Was anyone else in or near the kitchen?" I ask.

"The entire bridal party was just outside it, talking."

More like waiting until the coast was clear so they could steal the wine. And they were only able to steal one bottle because Haley came into the kitchen.

"Can we see Drew Bloom's room?" I ask since it doesn't look like there's anything left in this room to help me figure out why anyone would want these people dead.

"Sure. Follow me." Elena brings us directly across the hall. This room is smaller than the others. There's only one bed.

"Drew was the only occupant of this room?" I asked.

"He requested a single room, yes."

Because he didn't have a date or because he didn't really know anyone else here other than the bride? Yet for some reason, Drew agreed to go to S.C. Tunney's with Donovan, Joseph, and their dates on Friday night. Why? Did he really know Jess would also be there?

I need to talk to Jess again and find out more about her relationship with Drew. But that needs to wait until after I search Drew's room. Just like with the previous room, any personal belongings have been removed. There's a stain on the floor near the bed, indicating that's where Drew dropped his drink when he died.

"What are you thinking?" Cam asks me.

"That there's virtually no evidence. No motive. No nothing." Is this how Quentin feels when I one-up him on a case? It's completely frustrating. I know I'm not a detective, and I haven't been trained to solve murders, but I feel like I should have stumbled across something useful by now.

"The police haven't found anything either. They're completely stumped. I have a feeling this case might go unsolved. And in the meantime, the killer is staying under my roof. I know it's probably silly, but I worry about Mother. She's so vulnerable in her room." Elena wraps her arms around her midsection as if giving herself a supportive hug. "None of these people has a reason to harm a sickly old woman they don't know, but I can't help being concerned."

"Of course, you can't," I say. "But at least you and your mother are rooming together for the time being." I'm sure they're locking up the room tightly at night, too.

"I really should go check on Mother before I head back downstairs," she says, exiting the room.

"I want to talk to Jessica again," I tell Cam. "Something tells me her relationship with Drew is the key to figuring out this case."

"We don't know which room is hers," Cam says.

"Then let's start knocking on doors." I walk out of Drew's room and knock on the door next to his.

Paige answers. "Yes?" Her tone isn't the friendliest, but considering she's basically on lockdown here until Quentin or I figure out the case, I can't blame her for not being pleasant.

"Hi, Paige. I was wondering if you could tell me which room Jessica is staying in."

"She's at the end of the hallway, but I think she's with

Nina right now. That's the one on the right before Jess and Xander's room." She points and then promptly closes the door in my face.

"Thanks for your help," I say to the closed door.

Cam shakes his head. "I guess she's tired of all this."

"I think we all are. Three days of no leads will do that to you." I walk up to Nina's door and knock.

Nina answers, leaning against the doorframe to deny entry to the room. "Can I help you?"

"We're looking for Jessica. Paige said she was here."

Nina jerks her head back, motioning behind her. "She's lying down right now."

"Is she awake?"

"Yes, but she's resting. She just got back from speaking with the police. Can I help you instead?"

"Actually, no. We really need to talk to Jessica. May we come in for a few minutes, please?"

"It's fine, Nina. Let them in." Jessica appears behind her. Her eyes are red like she's been crying.

"Could we talk in private? Maybe in your room?" I ask her.

"You're welcome to talk in front of Nina. She's my best friend. I don't keep secrets from her." Jessica takes a seat at the end of one of the queen-size beds.

"Where's your roommate?" I ask Nina, who finally steps aside to let us into the room.

"April is in Paige's room with the others."

I assume the others means the rest of the bridal party.

Nina shuts the door behind Cam. I expect her to make a flirtatious comment or wink at him again, but she does neither.

"Jessica, we're trying to figure out Drew's place in all of this. We understand he was your friend and there might have been some tension when he came without a date." I'm trying to put it as mildly as possible so I don't set her off.

Jessica sniffles. "I've known Drew for years. He's always been nice to me."

"That's because he was in love with you," Nina says.

"Stop it. He got confused. That's all."

"What do you mean?" I ask, my gaze volleying between the two women.

Jessica lets out a deep breath. "Drew was always complimenting me. Any time I needed something, he was there. He was a good friend. But when he came here on Friday, he cornered me and asked me to end the engagement."

"Because he was in love with you and couldn't stand to see you marry someone else," Nina says.

"I think he was just afraid that our relationship would change if I got married."

"Why are you being so calm and understanding about this now?" Nina asks her. "You were so upset on Friday. That's why you asked Xander to have Donovan and Joseph take Drew out with them on Friday night. You wanted to get Drew away from you."

Well, there's one mystery solved. Thank you, Nina.

"Do either of you happen to know how they convinced Drew to go along with them since he didn't even really know them?"

Nina bobs one shoulder. "I'm pretty sure they implied we'd all be going there. Drew was most likely under the impression that he was hitching a ride with them."

I'm starting to think we're on a roll now. "And how was Drew when they got back Friday night?"

Jessica reaches for a tissue from the box next to her on the bed. "I didn't see him. We were all in Paige, Laura, and Justine's room. Since that's where half the bridal party is staying, it's sort of become the party room." She blows her nose loudly.

"So you didn't see Drew until the next day?"

"That's right. At breakfast, Drew asked me why I didn't sit with everyone at the restaurant. Xander and I had a private table for two. I thought seeing me happy with Xander would help Drew understand he didn't have a shot with me." Jessica tosses her tissue into the garbage can next to the desk in the corner of the room.

"And how did Drew react?"

"He was angry. Really angry. Said I set the whole thing up and lied to him."

He was right about that.

"What did you say to that?" Cam asks.

"He wouldn't even give me the opportunity to explain. He stormed off, and I didn't see him again until the party that night. I went over to his table to talk to him, but—"

"When was that?" I ask.

"Um, I guess right before we got the wine."

That could mean that Jessica got Drew angry, and he decided to poison the drinks I was busy making at the time. But that still leaves the question of why he'd drink one, too, unless he really didn't think he could live without Jessica.

"How did he react when you spoke to him?" Cam asks.

"He said he wanted things to go back to the way they were. I told him I wanted the same thing. But instead of being happy about that, he got angry. He said I didn't understand."

Yeah, because he was probably talking about before Jessica was engaged, and that wasn't at all what she was saying. Was she really that oblivious to his feelings for her? If so, I might have another Samantha on my hands.

"That's when I came over and got Jess out of there," Nina says. "I noticed Xander eyeing them at the table. I didn't want to see Drew ruin the evening, so I pulled Jess away with some urgent bridal party thing."

"And that's when you guys went to get some wine to bring back to your room." I fill in the gap for her.

"Right," Nina says.

"Nina's always bailing me out when I'm in trouble," Jessica says. "That's why she's my maid of honor." Jessica reaches for Nina's hand and squeezes it.

I can't think of anything else to ask either woman, so

I say, "Thank you both for speaking with us. We'll let you rest now." I turn and walk out with Cam on my heels.

Once we're in the hallway with the door shut, I say, "Drew was angry enough to pull this off."

"You mean he poisoned the couples for tricking him Friday night and then killed himself to avoid having to live without Jess?" Cam asks.

I nod. "And if that's really the case, we'll never be able to prove it since the only proof will have died with Drew."

CHAPTER EIGHT

Cam and I head back to Cup of Jo to check on Jamar and to meet Robin, our newest employee. Jamar sent me a text saying she was there and he was already training her. The place is pretty quiet, but given it's just about closing time, that's not unusual.

Robin is at the register getting a tutorial from Jamar when we approach. She's a pretty girl. I'd guess she's the same age as Jamar, about mid-twenties. She's tall and slender with wavy brown hair and dark brown eyes to match. She finishes her sale and then looks up at me.

"You must be Ms. Coffee," she says, extending her hand. "I'm Robin."

I shake her hand. "You can call me Jo. Jamar speaks very highly of you."

She turns her head to smile at him. "Jamar's a sweetheart. I don't think I've ever heard him say a bad word about anyone."

I have. Specifically about Quentin. Not that I can blame him there. "This is my boyfriend and business partner, Camden Turner."

"Cam," he says, extending his hand.

"It's nice to meet you both. Thank you for giving me a shot here. I hated working at the gym, and Jamar told me you two are great bosses."

"I haven't really gotten to show her how to make many drinks yet," Jamar says. "She's mostly been serving, cleaning tables, and ringing up orders. She's great with the register."

"No problem. I can show you how to make the drinks tomorrow morning. Why don't you two head out?"

Jamar consults his watch. "It's not five o'clock yet."

"That's okay. It's close enough." I grab the money from the tip jar, quickly count it, and distribute it evenly into two piles. "Here you go." I hand each a stack of bills.

Robin's eyes widen. "Wait. You're not keeping any?"

"I wasn't here serving. That money belongs to you two."

"Told you she's great," Jamar says.

"Thank you," Robin says with a huge smile as she takes her share of the tips. "I'll see you bright and early tomorrow." She's still smiling as Jamar walks her out. He waves to Cam and me as the door closes.

"She seems nice," Cam says.

"I knew Jamar wouldn't recommend anyone he

didn't think would work out." I immediately start cleaning the coffee machines for the day.

Cam goes to the kitchen to clean up and prep for the next day. In about thirty minutes, we're ready to head out.

Mo's just walking in as we're grabbing our things to leave. "Hey. I found something you might be interested in."

"What's that?"

She pulls out her phone and taps the screen. "A very public dispute between the best man and the two groomsmen who were murdered."

"Public as in online?" Who is stupid enough to engage in an online fight these days?

Mo turns the screen to me. "Apparently, Donovan and Joseph weren't happy that Xander chose Owen for best man over them. It started a fight among Donovan, Joseph, and Owen, which then sparked another fight between Joseph and Owen over Haley."

"Because Owen dated Haley before Joseph," I say.

"Right."

I quickly scan the comments in the post. "They certainly don't mask their feelings."

"Guys tend to just lay it all out there," Cam says.

"What if Owen poisoned the drinks to get back at Donovan, Joseph, and Haley?" Mo asks.

"That would make Lena an innocent bystander," I say. "Whether or not he wanted to kill Drew as well is up in the air, though. I mean we know Xander didn't like

Drew. So maybe Owen thought he was doing Xander a favor by killing him, too."

"I think we should talk to Owen again tomorrow," Cam says.

"I think you're right, but it's not going to be easy considering how upset he got with us the last time we talked to him."

"That could be because you were getting too close to pinning this on him," Mo says. "If you were asking the right questions, it would make him get defensive."

She could be right about that. What is it with circles of friends having so many secrets? I'm starting to think most of the guests don't even like each other.

"Are you coming over for dinner?" I ask Mo.

"Not tonight. Wes is taking me out."

I like Wes, but I worry about how quickly things are moving with him and Mo. I don't want to be the overprotective big sister who is constantly warning her to be careful with her heart, but after what I've been through in the past, it's hard not to intervene.

"Call me later, and let me know how it goes," I tell her.

She eyes me suspiciously. "Do you not like Wes?"

"Why would you ask me that? Of course, I like him."

She cocks her head, unsure of whether to believe me. "Just checking. See you tomorrow."

Cam locks up the shop behind us. "I'm heading home to shower."

"Coming by afterward?" I ask him.

"As long as you want me to."

"Well, that's a silly thing to say. I always want to see you."

He leans down to kiss me. "See you in a bit."

I start for my car when I notice Samantha come out of Bouquets of Love with mascara running down her cheeks. Maybe it's because we used to be best friends or maybe it's because I hate to see people cry, but I can't stop my feet from moving in her direction. "Are you okay?" I ask her.

She flings her arms around me. "Oh, Jo. I don't know what to do."

Did something happen between her and Quentin? I cannot be their relationship therapist. That's asking way too much.

She pulls away and looks into my eyes. "I screwed up."

"How?"

"I took an order. A big one. For a wedding." She's breathing so heavily her words are coming out choppy.

"Breathe, Samantha. Breathe." I mimic taking several deep, even breaths, and she does the same.

"Can we sit down and talk over some coffee?" She gestures to Cup of Jo.

"I've already cleaned the machines for the night," I say, but when she starts sobbing all over again, I quickly add, "but sure. Come on." I open the shop and turn on the espresso machine. "What would you like?"

"How about a frappe with a chocolate stick in it?"

Sure, pick a drink that takes time to make since I have to cool the espresso. And I'll have to rewash the blender when I'm finished. I shoot off a quick text to Cam to let him know what's going on and promising to call him when I'm finished here. Since he's driving, I know it will take him a bit to respond.

I make the frappes while Sam sits at a table and cries. I'll have to clean her tears from the table when she leaves, too. Once I have the drinks made, I place a chocolate stick in each and bring them to the table. "Here you go. Now tell me what's going on."

"I thought I was going to lose a big order for flowers because it's for the wedding that Quentin is investigating."

He's not investigating a wedding, but I know what she means, so I motion for her to continue.

"I got a call, saying all the centerpieces should be black carnations. At first, I thought it was odd to have black flowers for a wedding, but I figured they were going with a black and white theme. Or they like penguins."

I resist the urge to roll my eyes because only Samantha would think someone would have a penguin-themed wedding. "Okay, so what happened?"

"The bride called me today after I sent her the invoice, and she was screaming about the flower color. She called me stupid and told me to cancel the entire order."

"Did you tell her someone called and requested the flowers be black?"

"I tried. She said I must have confused the weddings because she didn't call me. And now I have no idea which wedding wanted the black carnations. I might lose another client if I can't figure it out." She goes into hysterics again.

Knowing Samantha, it's entirely possible she mixed up two orders. And given the situation Jessica is in right now, I can see her blowing up at Samantha about a screwup like this. "How many weddings do you have coming up?" I ask.

"June is a big wedding month. I have seven orders placed. I just lost this one, but that leaves six others that I have to look into."

"Can't you check the invoices? You just said that's how this mistake was discovered."

Samantha shakes her head. "I don't usually put all the details on the invoices. I put them in the computer for myself."

Not exactly smart, but Samantha does things her own way. She always has. Most people overlook her blunders because she's cute and has a sweet personality. If she noted the flower color on the wrong invoice, she probably couldn't use the other invoices to figure out the mistake.

"Then, I'd try confirming the color choices with the other brides. Pass it off as procedure to follow-up and make sure everything is confirmed well ahead of time."

Samantha bobs her head. "I can do that."

"And from now on, I'd put all the specifics right on the invoice. That way you have them in two places and can easily confirm them. If they ever don't match, you'll know there's a problem. And if a customer signs an invoice with incorrect information, they can't really get too upset with you because they signed off on it. It will be just as much their fault for not carefully reading the invoice."

"You're smart, Jo." She wipes her damp cheek, smearing her mascara even more.

A knock on the door makes me look up. Quentin is standing outside on the sidewalk. I wave him inside.

Samantha quickly dabs at her face with a napkin, trying to clean herself up. "I'm probably a mess."

"Sam, sweetie, are you all right?" Quentin rushes over to her.

She nods. "Jo helped me. I'll be fine. It's just work stuff."

Quentin gives me a questioning look, probably as surprised as I am that I'm trying to help Samantha given the tension between the three of us.

I stand up and grab a cap for Samantha's to-go cup. "Here." I hand it to her.

"Thank you again, Jo."

I nod, and Quentin does something completely unexpected. He mouths, "Thank you," as he leads Samantha out of the shop.

"I can't believe how nice you are to those people," Mo says. "I couldn't do it." She caps her coffee and grabs the bag with two donuts I just placed on the counter for her.

"I'm a glutton for punishment obviously."

"No, it's called you're a good person," Cam says, quickly kissing my cheek before heading back inside the kitchen.

"Are you going to talk to the best man again today?" Mo asks me.

"That's the plan. I have to train Robin first, though." I gesture to her wiping down a table in the corner.

Mo eyes her up. "Do me a favor and keep her away from Wes. She's too pretty."

"Are you and Wes exclusive?" I ask.

"I think so. I mean, I'm not seeing anyone else, and he doesn't seem to be."

If she's not sure, then maybe things aren't as serious as I thought. "Well, whether you are or aren't, he'd be a jerk to hit on one of your sister's employees."

She leans on the counter. "Do you think he's a jerk? Am I being played?"

"Why are you suddenly questioning him? Did something happen?"

"I think it's the research for this case you're trying to solve. Friends fighting over women. People trying to stop weddings. Why does it have to be so hard?"

"The weird thing is I remember seeing the way Jessica and Xander looked at each other at that engagement party. I thought they were so in love."

"And now you're not so sure?"

I bob one shoulder. "I don't know. It could be the stress of the case making them fight. I mean their friends were murdered, and it's most likely that one of their remaining friends is the killer. That would put stress on any couple, right?"

Mo nods and sips her coffee. "Maybe I'm reading too much into things. Wes hasn't done anything to make me question him. I'm probably being unfair."

"How was your date last night? You never called me afterward."

"It was good. We went to dinner and a movie. Then he drove me home and kissed me goodnight. It was late so I crawled right into bed. And speaking of being late, I'm going to be late for work if I don't get out of here."

Mo works directly across the street, so it will take her all of two minutes to get to her office.

"Go on. Get out of here. Enjoy your breakfast with Wes," I say, knowing the second donut is for him.

She smiles at me and walks out.

"I'm ready to learn how to make drinks," Robin says, coming over to me.

"Great. You can shadow me this morning," I tell her.

At midday, Cam and I head out to talk to Owen. Robin and Jamar have things under control, and I feel a lot better about leaving when I know there are two people taking care of Cup of Jo.

When we get to the Reede B&B, I spot Quentin's

patrol car out front. "This can't be good," I say, getting out of the car.

"You really want him to know you're investigating?" Cam asks me.

More like I need to know what brought Quentin here today, so I don't have any other choice. I open the front door.

Quentin and another officer are inside talking to Elena. Elena looks up at me. "Oh, Jo. I'm so glad you're here."

Quentin, on the other hand, doesn't look happy to see me. "I thought you were staying away from this case?"

"I'm just visiting my friend Elena," I say.

Elena nods. "Jo and I have grown close over the past few months. She's been checking on me since this awful incident happened."

"Sure, she has." Quentin clears his throat.

"Want to tell me what's going on?" I ask them.

"The best man is missing," Elena says, much to Quentin's dismay. "No one has seen him since last night."

My prime suspect ran.

CHAPTER NINE

Cam and I exchange a look. Fleeing definitely makes Owen look guilty. We already know he was in the kitchen talking to Haley after I made the drinks. He had the means to poison the frappes. He also had motive if he was trying to get back at Joseph and Haley for dating each other when Owen was still hung up on Haley.

"Can I speak with you for a moment, Jo?" Quentin says, motioning in the direction of the library. "Keep everyone else in the living room," he tells the other officer, who gives a curt nod in response.

Cam starts to follow, but Quentin holds up a hand to stop him.

"It's fine," I tell Cam. He doesn't look happy to leave me alone with Quentin, but he doesn't question me either.

Quentin makes me lead the way even though he's the

one who wants this private meeting. I enter the library and turn to face him. "What's this about?"

"Sam told me about last night. What you did for her. You didn't have to." He clears his throat. "I wanted to thank you."

"You already thanked me for that. What's this really about?"

He huffs. "Fine. Since you can't seem to keep your nose out of my cases, I'm interested in hearing what you've got so far."

I'm getting nowhere, at least not with Owen gone, so I might as well fill him in. "I came here to talk to Owen." I tell him my reasons for suspecting him.

"That's good. He's the first person who seems to have motive and opportunity. And the fact that he ran during an ongoing investigation makes him a person of interest."

"Agreed. But how do you plan to track him down?" I ask. "The families are arriving today. I'm sure you're going to be swamped trying to talk to them."

He starts pacing as he thinks. "I can put out an APB on him while I talk to the families of the victims."

"Why did you rule me out as a suspect?" I ask him. "And better yet, how did you convince the BFPD not to pursue me?"

"You've helped us with cases before. It gives you some credibility with the BFPD. The fact that you didn't know any of the victims means you have no motive. Plus, you'd be sabotaging your own business. In truth, no one thought you were guilty. I questioned Elena Reede based on a rumor that she wants to get rid of the B&B. But no one mentioned seeing her near the drinks in the kitchen on the night of the murders. Plenty of witnesses have her at the party itself."

Except she *was* in the kitchen. Did she lie to Quentin about that? And if so, was it out of fear? Or has she been nice to me because she's playing me, trying to get me to help cover for her?

"I know that look. What are you thinking, Jo?"

The last thing I want to do is cover for a killer. "I'm not saying I think she did this because I really don't think she did."

"Who?"

"Elena Reede told me she was in the kitchen getting ice for the bridal party."

"I know," he says. "The bridal party told me as much, but they also saw her the entire time. She didn't go near the drinks."

That's good to know. I didn't realize the bridal party was keeping that close of an eye on her at the time. "Then I guess we're back to Owen being the most likely suspect."

"Looks that way." He starts to walk out, but I call after him.

"Please don't tell Elena I mentioned she was in the kitchen. She's finally being nice to me after the last case that brought us here."

"You didn't tell me anything I didn't already know, so I see no reason to mention it to her." He walks out.

Cam comes into the library and cocks his head at me, his way of asking what happened.

"I just told him what we found out about Owen. He's putting out an APB on him so he can focus on talking to the families of the victims today."

"When are they arriving?"

"I'm not sure, but I'm assuming they'll go straight to the station when they get here."

"What's your next move since you can't talk to Owen?"

There's only one thing I can think to do. "I want to talk to Xander. I'm assuming of the people here, he knows Owen best."

"He's in the living room with the others."

"We'll wait until Quentin and his partner leave. Then we'll ask Xander to come talk to us away from everyone else."

We only have to wait about twenty minutes before we get the opportunity to talk to Xander. He looks shaken when he steps into the library. He takes a seat in a high-backed chair and immediately puts his head in his hands.

After a minute or two, he raises his head and looks at us. "I'm not sure how this got so screwed up. I'm supposed to be at work right now, but we're all trapped here, being treated as suspects."

"Do you know why Owen left?" I ask.

"No. He didn't tell me he was planning to leave. He didn't tell anyone."

"When was the last time you spoke to him?" I take a step closer to him.

"I guess at dinner. They ordered pizzas for us since the kitchen is still closed. I sat next to Owen. He seemed normal. Never mentioned anything about leaving."

"Did he say anything about Haley after she died?" I ask.

Xander picks up his head. "He told you about him and her?"

"Yeah. He said they used to date, and he was upset that she showed up with Joseph."

"He also said he went into the kitchen to talk to Haley in private the night of the party," Cam adds.

Xander's eyes widen. "And that made you think he poisoned the drinks, didn't it? Is that why the police are looking into him?"

"The police are looking into everyone," I say. "Us included." I gesture to Cam and me. "Everyone who was here Saturday night has to be questioned."

"I know. It's just all too much. These are my friends."

"Except for Drew," I say.

Xander scoffs. "Don and Joseph tried to keep him away from Jess. She's different when he's around. When it's just her and me, things are great. But..."

"From what we've found out, Jessica was upset with Drew. One theory is that Drew poisoned your friends and himself because he was angry and couldn't deal with the upcoming wedding."

"Wouldn't he poison me to get me out of the way? I was the one standing between him and Jess. Why kill Don and Joseph?" Xander shakes his head. "It just doesn't make sense."

How do I tell him his group of close friends doesn't make much sense? "Xander, all I know is your friends have secrets that keep coming out as we look into things. People who don't seem to be linked turn out to be. Like Joseph, Haley, and Owen. If there are any other secrets you know about that we don't, you need to tell us."

Xander swallows so hard I see it. "Nothing I know about."

He's lying. He knows something. He just doesn't want to say it.

I take a step closer to him. "Do you want to know who killed your friends?"

"Of course, I do."

"Then you need to talk to us. I can tell you're hiding something."

He stands up. "I'm not hiding anything. I admitted that Owen was upset about Haley and Joseph. And I admitted I didn't like Drew. I don't like talking about this stuff. Two of my friends were killed and now another is missing. If you think I'm acting odd, tell me how I'm supposed to act after all that?" When Cam and I don't respond, Xander scoffs and storms out of the room.

I walk over to the bookcase and lean my elbow on it. "He's keeping something from us."

"Is it possible he knows who the killer is?" Cam asks.

I'm not sure if he knows or has his suspicions. The way the groomsmen and bridal party are keeping to themselves and away from the other guests, who have entirely blended into the background on this case, makes me very suspicious. "We need to talk to the other guests. The ones we've passed over for not being close enough to Xander and Jessica or the wedding parties."

"You want to interview everyone."

"I think we have to. We can quickly rule out those who were nowhere near the kitchen or the table whose drinks were poisoned. But more than that, we can find out if any of them know about the secrets circulating among the wedding party."

"I see. Find out what rumors were going around. That's a good idea. And since Owen isn't here to talk to, it will keep us moving forward so this day isn't a complete waste."

"Exactly." I consider everything I've learned about these so-called friends. They've been friends for years, which means they know a lot about each other, including how to keep things from each other. But talking to them all might allow us to piece a few things together because it's clear these people know a lot more than they're saying.

CHAPTER TEN

Cam and I spend the rest of the day talking to every guest, finding out where they sat, who they talked to, if they went into the kitchen at any time, and if they visited the table where the poisoned drinks were served. We tackle the list of people separately to cover more ground in less time. I stick to the library, while Cam questions people in the living room. Luckily, they're all under the impression that Cam and I are consulting with the BFPD on this case, so they're cooperating with us.

"How long have you known Jessica and Xander?" I ask a woman in her thirties named Erica.

"Oh, I work with Jessica at the library. I don't know Xander really well at all."

"How long have you worked together?"

"I'd say about six months now."

"Do you ever hang out outside of work?"

"Of course. We have the same lunch break, so we usually go grab something to eat together."

"Would you say you're close?" I cross my legs in the high-backed chair.

"I guess as close as colleagues get. We talk about things, but we don't really confide in each other about anything of real significance, if you know what I mean."

"So she doesn't talk about her relationship with Xander?"

"She mentions things they do together. You know, restaurants they go to, movies they see. She raved about this restaurant. I think it was called the Bella Dona. It was hours away. Just stuff like that."

"Do you know any of the other guests here?"

"Just Cherise. She works at the library, too. We're rooming together along with our dates."

"Well, thank you for your time. If you wouldn't mind, could you send Cherise in here next?"

"Sure thing." She stands up from her chair and walks out.

Cam comes into the library, looking a little defeated. "Are you getting the feeling that no family was invited to this thing for a reason?"

"What do you mean?"

"Well, the entire guest list is under thirty-five. Yet they chose a bed and breakfast for the location. Why?"

It turned out to be a good location to commit murder. "Maybe there's another engagement party for the families," I suggest.

"I guess that's possible. Did you find out anything useful?"

"Not yet. I'm guessing you haven't either."

"Nope. Not a thing. These people are basically acquaintances. I feel like they were only invited because it meant more gifts."

Speaking of gifts... "Where are the gifts? Have they been opened?"

"I'm assuming in Xander and Jessica's room. Why?"

"I don't know. I just haven't given them any thought until you just mentioned them."

"Do you think they're important?"

"Probably not." The gift table at the party was mostly cards. I highly doubt the killer would send a card with a message that their gift is in the form of five dead bodies.

A woman steps into the library. "Hi, Erica said you wanted to speak with me. I'm Cherise."

"Come in, Cherise," I say.

Cam gives me a wave and heads out to interview more guests.

I go through the same line of questioning all over again.

"Jess didn't really talk about her personal life much. When we'd get bored shelving books, we'd talk about good places to eat or which stores were having good sales. This one time, she took the day off from work and went to the city. She came back with this great pair of boots and said she had the best meal of her life."

"Was that at Bella Dona's? Erica mentioned it."

"I think so. But really that's as well as I know Jessica. I was kind of surprised she invited me to this party, but I just figured she must not have many friends." She bobs one shoulder and gives a half smile. "It's kind of sad."

Once all the interviews are finished, I meet up with Cam in the lobby area.

"I'm beat," I tell him.

"I'm right there with you. I'm convinced there are two groups of people at this bed and breakfast: those who know Xander and Jessica extremely well, and those who barely know them at all."

We stop talking when a group comes into the lobby.

"I think it's a great idea," Nina says, walking toward the stairs with Xander and Jessica.

"It seems a little callous to me," Xander says, pausing with his hand on the railing.

"Some of those gifts are from Donavan, Joseph, and even Drew. They're the last things they gave you. Opening them might actually make you feel a little bit better right now. You know, make it feel like they're still here." Nina offers them a sympathetic smile.

"You're right," Jessica says. "And maybe it will lighten everyone's spirits. "Let's bring them down and do this in the living room so everyone can be there."

"How weird is it that we were talking about the gifts earlier, and now they're going to open them?" I ask Cam.

"It is a little coincidental. Do you think someone overheard us?"

"I don't know. Maybe." We head for the living room

since that's where they're bringing the gifts. For some reason, I want to see them. Maybe it will give us some insight into who these people really are.

Xander walks in carrying a stack of wrapped gifts, while Jessica carries a woven basket with envelopes inside. They take a seat on the couch with everyone else standing or sitting around them.

"Which one first?" Jessica asks, and I get the impression she really likes presents because she's smiling as if she doesn't have a care in the world.

"I don't care. You pick," Xander says.

"Don't be a party pooper, Xander. We're trying to lighten everyone's spirits, remember?" She leans over and kisses his cheek, and he nods in response.

Xander picks up a wrapped gift about the size of a shoebox and hands it to Jessica. "You do the honors."

"Hang on." Nina gets her phone ready to take pictures.

"Oh, good thinking, Nina. Thank you," Jessica says.

"That's what the maid of honor is for. Read the card first."

Jessica opens the card taped to the top of the box. "It's from Madeline."

Cam must have interviewed her because I have no idea which one of these people is Madeline.

Jessica opens the box and pulls out two champagne flutes.

"I thought you could use them at the wedding," a woman in the back of the room says.

"They're beautiful. You even had them engraved with our names. Thank you, Madeline."

The next gift is a set of silver candlesticks. Do people even really use those anymore? They also get a fancy coffee maker that even has me drooling over it. Then they move on to the cards.

Most of them contain money or checks, the typical gifts to put inside cards. Jess reads each one aloud before placing the check or money back inside and returning the cards to their envelopes. When she reaches the card from Donovan she gets choked up.

"I'm sorry. I thought this would make us all feel better, but knowing they're gone…" She starts to cry, and Nina rushes to get her a tissue.

"We can do this another time," Xander says.

"No. I want to do this. They were our friends."

She didn't even like Donovan. If his card is making her so upset, what will seeing Joseph's and Drew's do to her?

She blows her nose and hands the used tissue back to Nina, who, to her credit, takes it in stride, placing it inside a clean tissue and then disposing of it in the small trash can in the corner of the room. Nina gets her phone ready to record once again, and Jess gives her a small nod to let her know she's ready to continue.

She reads the card, and when she gets to the final line, which reads, "I love you both," she's full on sobbing again.

Xander wraps his arm around her shoulders and

cries with her. Nina rushes to get more tissues for them both.

Cam and I step just outside the living room. I feel like we were intruding on a private moment. We don't even know these people, and to see them this upset feels too personal.

"I guess Jessica is feeling guilty for the way she spoke about Donovan when we first questioned her. She was pretty harsh about his dating habits, and there he is telling her and Xander he loves them in the card."

"I can't imagine any of this is easy." I look around the room. There's not a dry eye in the place. I can't see any of these people having committed murder, which must mean Owen is the culprit. It has to be why he ran away. Hopefully, the BFPD finds him soon, and this can all be over.

It takes a few minutes for everyone to collect themselves. I'm surprised they haven't dispersed to their rooms, but Jessica reaches for another card.

"This one is from Erica and Cherise," she says. She reads the card aloud. "Because you both had the best meal of your lives there, we wanted to send you back to repeat the experience."

Xander leans closer to Jess, his eyes narrowed. "Bella Dona? Where's that?"

I move closer to the library to see the looks on Cherise's and Erica's faces. They're whispering back and forth, seemingly confused.

"Did we get the name wrong?" Cherise asks.

Jess quickly closes the card. "I think you did, but that's okay. It's a very thoughtful gift, and I'm sure we'll enjoy the meal. Thank you." She immediately reaches for another card.

I pull Cam back out into the hallway. "Did you see that?"

"She recognized the name of the restaurant," he says. "I could see it in her expression."

"I know. And both Erica and Cherise told me Jessica raved about the place. She even took a day off work to go there."

"Yet Xander didn't know the restaurant," Cam says.

"So who did Jess go there with?" Because it sure wasn't her beloved fiancé.

CHAPTER ELEVEN

I get home to find an unwanted guest on my doormat.

"Quentin, what are you doing here?" I step around him to unlock the door as he stands up.

"I'd rather tell you inside." He motions to my apartment.

"Let me explain how this works. You wait to be invited in. You don't order me into my own apartment to talk to you."

"May I come in?" he asks through clenched teeth.

"I suppose. There's actually something I want to talk to you about, but you go first." I step inside and toss my keys onto the kitchen counter. I usually leave my door open so Midnight can wander in, but Quentin closes it behind him.

He clears his throat before he begins. "We found something in Donovan Shepherd's pocket. We didn't think anything of it at first, but when his family came to retrieve his personal belongings today, they said it didn't belong to Donovan. It belongs to Jessica Scanlon."

"What was it?" I ask, wondering why Donovan would have something of Jessica's. Jessica didn't even seem like she liked Donovan.

"Her class ring."

I grab two bottles of water from the refrigerator and hand one to him. "Like a high school class ring?"

He nods and lowers his head as he takes the bottle. I know what he's thinking. We exchanged class rings for a while as well. Only we gave them back after we broke up.

"So you think Donovan and Jessica dated at some point," I say.

"It seems that way, but I don't have any confirmation yet."

"Maybe not confirmation, but I have a story for you that might fit that scenario really well."

He leans against the counter and opens the water bottle. "Go on."

"Okay, when Cam and I first talked to Jessica, she didn't seem to have a high opinion of Donovan. She made it a point to mention how he's a serial dater, and no one knew the woman Lena that he brought to the party. She seemed bitter about it, and I wrote it off as Jessica not being a fan of guys who date lots of women."

"Makes sense."

"Until today, when Jessica was opening the engagement gifts and read the card from Donovan.

Before signing the card, he wrote 'I love you both.' When Jessica read that line, she fell into a fit of hysterics."

"Do you think he really meant that he loved her?"

"I didn't at first. I thought maybe she felt guilty for speaking so poorly about him earlier. Until Jessica opened the next card, which was from two coworkers at the library."

"You know her coworkers? How much investigating did you manage to do behind my back?" He takes a swig from his water bottle.

"Is that really what you want to discuss right now? I'm about to piece this together for you."

He tips the bottle slightly in my direction, indicating I have the floor.

"Inside the card was a gift card to a restaurant called Bella Dona. When I talked to the two coworkers—separately, I should mention—they each brought up how Jessica raved about that restaurant. She took the day off from work to go shopping in the city, and that's where she had the best meal she's ever eaten."

"Okay? Why is that helpful?" Quentin asks.

"Because Xander had never heard of Bella Dona."

Quentin stands up straight, his eyes widening in the process. "Which means she didn't go with him."

"No. I think she went with Donovan."

"So they were having an affair."

"It sure looks that way after what you found out about the class ring."

"We need to get her to confirm that."

I furrow my brow at him. "We? You want me to talk to Jessica, don't you?"

"You've successfully roadblocked me in this town, Jo. After the scene at S.C. Tunney's, no one wants to talk to me."

In other words, he can't solve this case without me. "What makes you think Jessica will talk to me?"

"So far, who have you talked to who hasn't answered your questions?"

No one. But again, I don't have a badge. I'm not as threatening, and one of these people is a killer. "Okay, I'll talk to Jessica. Based on what she told me about Donovan being a serial dater, I'm willing to believe she had a lot of animosity toward him. He probably cheated on her." I level Quentin with a look.

"No amount of apologizing will ever make you stop throwing that in my face, will it?"

"As a police detective, I'm sure you believe the punishment should fit the crime. No matter how many times you apologize, I still feel the sting of betrayal every time I see you or Samantha. It only seems fair you feel shame for it."

"Do you know how difficult it is to do my job when people in my hometown don't respect me?"

"Respect is something you earn, Detective. And when you have to earn it back after losing it, it's twice as hard. That's a lesson you're going to have to learn."

Quentin clears his throat. "Will you help me?"

It's just like him to change the subject. "Yes, I'll help

because it's entirely possible that Jessica poisoned Donovan and his date out of anger. The others might have been killed simply because Jessica couldn't predict which of the five frappes Donovan and Lena would drink from."

"Do you think she could have been working with the best man to pull this off?" he asks. "Why else would he run?"

"That's a good point. And killing Joseph and Haley benefited Owen since he was angry about them dating. It's entirely possible they were working together."

"That would leave Drew as the innocent one who got caught in the crossfire." He finishes his water and places the bottle on the counter by the sink where I keep my recycling.

"Innocent but not so innocent. He tried to ruin the party and end the engagement."

"Which is a lot better than murder," Quentin says.

"Did you learn anything else from the families of the victims?"

He leans back against the counter and crosses his ankles. "Not really. Lena's family didn't know Donovan at all. They're the most broken up about this because they feel like their daughter was killed by a complete stranger. A case of in the wrong place at the wrong time."

"Which is most likely true."

"Joseph's parents are both dead, so his uncle came to collect his belongings. That was the easiest one to deal with since he hadn't even talked to Joseph in years. They weren't close."

"What about Drew and Haley?" I ask.

"Haley's parents are divorced. Her mother showed up, totally shaken. Haley's sister was with her, though. She's a pretty tough girl. She held it together for the both of them."

"That leaves Drew."

"Drew's parents are odd. They said Drew loved Jessica, and he probably found peace in dying in her presence."

Except he died alone in his room. I guess Quentin kept that to himself to allow Drew's parents some sense of peace themselves.

"Alright, tomorrow I'll go talk to Jessica."

"I'm going with you. Leave Cam at Cup of Jo."

I hold up my free hand. "You can stop right there. You don't get to order my boyfriend around. He's been with me the entire time. I'm not leaving him behind now just because you decided you need my help."

"Jo, I'm not discussing this with you right now. This is my investigation. I get to call the shots."

"Fine. Count me out then." I finish my water and place the bottle on the counter. "Let me get the door for you."

"You're being unreasonable."

"Really? I thought I was being more than reasonable when I consoled your fiancée the other night. And I think I'm being very reasonable allowing you into my apartment to discuss yet another case you can't solve on your own."

"This is why we never would have worked out."

"That is not a road you want to go down, Detective." I open the door. "It's time for you to leave."

He glares at me before walking out. "I'll be at the B&B at nine. See you there."

"You'll see Cam and me there," I say, slamming the door behind him.

About ten seconds later, someone knocks on the door. I fling it open, ready to give Quentin a verbal lashing, but it's Jamar standing in the hallway.

"Whoa, don't shoot." He holds a hand in the air.

"Sorry, I thought you were a certain police detective."

"Thankfully, I'm not. Besides, you know I come bearing gifts." He pulls a pitcher of margaritas from behind his back.

"I think you just earned employee of the month," I say, holding out my arm to welcome him inside.

"What was Quentin doing here anyway?"

"Asking for my help, as usual."

Jamar laughs as he sets the pitcher down on the counter and gets two glasses.

"Make it three," I say as Cam appears in the doorway.

Jamar turns and waves at Cam. "Coming right up."

I throw my arms around Cam's neck. "Thank you for being you," I say.

"Why do I get the feeling Quentin was here?" he asks me.

"Because in addition to being exceptionally attractive, you're also very smart." I let go of him and reach for a freshly poured margarita.

Jamar hands one to Cam and takes the other for himself. "To a Quentin-free evening."

"Hear, hear!" I say, clinking my glass together with theirs.

Cam and I arrive at the Reede B&B at ten to nine. Jamar and Robin have Cup of Jo under control. Robin picked up on how to make the drinks really quickly. I suspect Jamar will be serving the customers, which suits him since he likes to dance with them in the process anyway. He's definitely a showman.

"Do you think Jamar and Robin will get together?" Cam asks me.

"I kind of hope not," I say.

"Why's that? I thought you liked Robin."

"I do, but if they break up, we'd probably end up losing an employee." I bump my shoulder into his as we walk into the B&B.

Quentin hasn't arrived yet, so the atmosphere in the B&B isn't as tense as I'm assuming it will get in a few minutes. We take advantage of that by seeking out Jessica on our own. We find her in the living room with her bridal party. Cam and I stay in the hallway to listen in on their conversation. I'm hoping they'll be more open if they don't know we're around.

"I don't understand why everything is going wrong. First the engagement party is ruined. Then the flowers are the wrong color. I mean how stupid does the woman at the florist have to be? No one orders black flowers for a wedding. And now this. The bridesmaids' dresses are all wrong."

Jess is turning into a real bridezilla if she thinks black flowers and the wrong dresses are worse than five people dying at her engagement party.

"Maybe you should consider postponing the wedding," Nina says.

"I can't. Everything is paid for. My parents would kill me," Jess says.

"But you and Xander aren't in a good place right now. I'd hate to see all of this ruin your special day. It's supposed to be perfect." She takes Jess's hands in hers. "Jess, I love you like a sister, and I want your wedding day to be the best day of your life. I'll handle all the arrangements. You won't have to worry about a thing. I promise. After a little time, you and Xander will get past all this and you'll remember why you fell in love with each other in the first place. Then we can pick back up with the wedding plans. Trust me. You'll be happy you waited."

"Nina has a point, Jess," April says. "With everything that's going on, none of this seems right. I mean Xander lost two close friends. You can't expect him to be himself for a while. He needs time to grieve."

"But—"

"Just talk to Xander about it," Nina says. "I'm sure you two can work something out."

It gets quiet, and I realize they're breaking up the little powwow. I pull Cam back toward the staircase.

"Jessica," I say as she walks out of the room. "Can we speak to you for a moment in the library?"

She doesn't look happy to see us. "It's early. I haven't even had any coffee yet. Can it wait?"

"It can, but just so you know, Detective Perry is on his way."

"Oh." She must think we're trying to give her a heads-up because she turns for the library without another moment's hesitation. "What does he want from me now?"

"I'll be honest with you. He found out something that I don't think you want your fiancé to know about."

She sinks into a chair, her face turning pale. "What does he know?"

I move closer and keep my voice down. "Were you having an affair with Donovan Shepherd?"

She buries her head in her hands.

"Jessica, we need to know the truth. If you let the police speculate about this, they're going to draw some really big conclusions that aren't going to make you look good." I bend down in front of her. "I'm trying to help you." Or catch her if she is the killer.

"It ended a month ago," she says, finally meeting my gaze. "You can't tell Xander. Please. I love him. He's the one I want to be with."

"Then why were you with Donovan?" I ask. I'll never understand cheaters. Never.

"Xander wanted me to get to know his friends. This was right after he proposed. So one night, his groomsmen took me out for drinks. Don and I stayed the latest and were doing shots at the bar. We got a little tipsy. The next thing I knew, we were kissing. The following day, I thought the whole thing would blow over, but when Don and I saw each other…I knew I was in trouble."

"So you kept seeing each other behind Xander's back," I say.

"We kept saying we were going to end it. For Xander's sake. But we had this connection. Or, at least, I thought we did. He told me he had this huge crush on me in high school, so I gave him my class ring and said if I'd known, maybe things would have been different."

Cam reaches for my hand and squeezes it. Their situation is undeniably similar to how Quentin and Sam got together while Quentin was with me. Luckily, we weren't engaged at the time. I give Cam a small smile to let him know I'm okay. It all worked out for the best.

Jessica's face gets red. "I couldn't believe he showed up here with another woman."

"She wasn't a decoy to make sure Xander didn't find out about you two?" I ask.

"I don't know. He didn't even discuss it with me. I

mean Drew came alone. Why couldn't Don? He could have said he wanted to party with his friends and decided against bringing a random date. But, instead, he brought that tramp."

She certainly sounds angry enough to kill right now.

"And then Drew found out about Don and me. He knew the second he saw me. He said the way I was looking at Don told the entire story."

"Did he threaten to tell Xander?" I ask.

"He told me I could call off the wedding and leave with him, or he'd out Don and me in front of everyone at brunch Sunday morning."

That's a pretty big motive to silence Drew.

"I was so angry I could've killed him for threatening me like that."

"So you did," Quentin says in the doorway. "Jessica Scanlon, you're under arrest for the murders of Donovan Shepherd, Lena Howard, Joseph Dunbar, Haley Roebuck, and Drew Bloom."

CHAPTER TWELVE

"No! I didn't kill anyone!" Jessica grips the armrests on the chair. "I never said that."

A crowd is gathering in the hallway, and Xander pushes his way to the front. "What's going on? Jess, are you okay?"

She jumps up. "Xander, don't listen to them. I didn't do anything."

Oh, she did plenty, but I'm not sure if she went as far as killing anyone.

"Hands behind your back," Quentin tells her.

"Xander, please. Do something. Tell them I'd never hurt any of our friends."

"Someone tell me what's going on here," Xander says.

"I'm taking your fiancée down to the station to book her," Quentin says.

"Quentin, I think you're jumping the gun here,"

I say.

"Jo, let me do my job." He cuffs Jessica and pushes her through the crowd in the hallway.

Elena eyes me as we walk by her. "Jo?"

I step toward her. "I'm not sure he's arresting the right person," I tell her. "Keep watching everyone closely. I wouldn't let your guard down just yet if I were you."

She nods.

"Are the rest of us free to go?" someone murmurs.

"Let's go," I tell Cam. "We need to follow them to the station. I have more questions for Jessica."

Quentin puts Jessica into the back of his patrol car. "Jo, go back to work. We're finished here."

"You might be, but I'm just getting started. Did you forget there's a missing best man? You told me last month that I can't dismiss details of a case just because it's convenient. Now I'm reminding you of the same thing. You're missing something." I get into Cam's SUV and close the door.

I can't hear Quentin, but I can read the curse that comes off his lips as he gets into the patrol car.

"You don't think she did this, do you?" Cam asks me.

"Not on her own. We have to account for everything, and a missing best man is too much to overlook."

"You think he helped her because he wanted Haley and Joseph to pay for dating each other."

"It's possible. We need to find him. I can't see why he'd run if he wasn't guilty of something."

"This is the most messed up group of friends ever."

At the station, we have to wait until Jessica is booked. Quentin is telling everyone she confessed and that Cam and I witnessed the confession. That's not what happened, though, and Jessica is screaming exactly that at everyone she encounters.

Finally, the chief calls Quentin into his office. I've never met the police chief, but I've heard he's not someone you mess with. When Quentin comes out of the office, he looks green. He walks over to Cam and me. "Chief Caswell wants to speak with you both. Just tell him you heard her confess."

"Quentin, she didn't confess. She said she wanted to kill Drew, but she didn't say she did. She was angry."

Quentin's jaw tightens. "Jo, if you go in there and say that, you could make me lose my badge."

"I'm not going to lie to the chief of police."

"You heard her. She confessed." His expression is a combination of anger and panic.

"That she wanted to kill him. She never confessed to poisoning anyone."

"You're trying to bury me, aren't you?"

Chief Caswell appears in his doorway, which he takes up with his huge, looming form. "Did she or didn't she confess?"

"She did," Quentin asserts.

"Chief, I think there's been a misunderstanding. Detective Perry walked in on what he thought was a confession, but I don't think he heard the entire conversation." I don't want to get Quentin fired. I'm not petty enough to ruin his career. "I think he did what he thought was best in the situation. I can see how what she said could be interpreted as a confession if you didn't witness the entire conversation."

"My office," the chief says. "All of you." He holds the door as we step inside. "From the start, tell me everything that happened."

I spend ten minutes rehashing my conversation with Jessica, and then I go silent.

The chief taps his pen on the desk. "She admitted to the affair and to being angry with two of the victims. She even admitted to wanting to kill one of them. Is that correct?"

"Yes, sir," I say.

"But she never actually admitted to the crime?"

"Not exactly, no."

"I see." He leans back in his chair. "Detective Perry, you have one hour to put that woman in an interrogation room and get a confession out of her. If you fail to do that, you will release her with an apology stating that you alone are to blame for her arrest."

"Yes, sir," Quentin says, already starting for the door.

"I'm not finished."

Quentin stops, and I swear I can hear his heart pounding in his chest.

"If you fail, you will serve a suspension for a period of one month. Do I make myself clear?"

"Yes, sir."

"Dismissed."

Quentin walks out, and I hurry after him with Cam right beside me.

"Quentin, wait. I think I can help."

"You've done enough."

I grab his arm and spin him around. "I'm not the one who jumped to conclusions. I had her talking. You never should have interrupted me. I was getting somewhere with her, but you couldn't handle that, and you took over. Your pride got you into this situation. Are you really going to let it interfere again now and make this worse?"

He shakes my hand off his arm.

"Let me go in there with you," I say.

"You only have one hour," Cam adds. "You need our help."

Quentin looks completely torn. Losing his badge, even if only for a month, would destroy him.

"You came to me for a reason. Let me help you," I say.

He groans, which I know is as good as a yes, so I follow him to an interrogation room.

"Wait here." He leaves us to get Jessica.

"What's your plan?" Cam asks.

"To find out just how much she knows."

"He's going to lose his badge when she doesn't confess."

"Most likely." I stop talking when the door opens.

Jessica walks in with her hands cuffed. "I didn't kill anyone."

"I don't think you did, but I think you have more to

tell us," I say, taking a seat at the small table. I gesture across from me, and she sits down. Cam takes the seat next to me, and Quentin remains standing in the doorway.

"I didn't confess to anything. Yes, I was angry and wanted to kill him, but I didn't." She sounds like a broken record.

"What did you do then?" I ask, needing her to move on.

"I talked to Nina. I tell her everything."

Everything? "Does she know about you and Don?"

Jess lowers her head, and at least she has the decency to look ashamed. "No. Not that. I didn't tell anyone about that. That's why I was so upset when Drew found out. Don and I were so careful."

"So you lied to Nina and told her Drew was just trying to get you to end the engagement."

"It wasn't really a lie. I just left out a lot of the truth."

That's called a lie by omission, but I need her to keep talking, so I don't correct her. "Okay. What happened after that?"

"The party was ending, so she told me we should go to the party room—Paige's room—as planned and see if Drew cooled off in the morning."

"You didn't see Drew or Don again after that?"

"No. We thought their entire table went to bed right after the party."

Really, they went up to their rooms and died, probably almost instantly.

"Do you know where Owen Pierce is? He had reason to want to harm Haley and Joseph."

She shakes her head. "No, I didn't see him either, but the groomsmen had their own party."

That's the first I'm hearing about that. How didn't they notice Joseph and Donovan were missing? "Did Xander say anything Sunday morning or even Saturday night about that party?"

"Not really, but the bodies were discovered Sunday morning and that took over all conversation."

"Jessica, can you think of anyone who would have wanted one of the five people dead?"

She sits back. "You've talked to all my friends. You know we're kind of a dysfunctional group."

"It's easier if you just spell this out at this point. I don't think you want to spend more time here than you have to."

She sits forward again. "Chris and Adam had it out for Owen. Jealousy, mainly."

"None of them is dead. Move on," Quentin says.

Jessica shoots him a death glare before returning her gaze to me.

"Everyone hated Drew. And Owen would do anything for Xander."

"Including kill for him?"

"If he did, I don't see why he'd kill Don and Joseph, though. Drew's honestly the most likely suspect."

"Except he's dead. Owen ran. Go back to him." Quentin must be eager to pin this on Owen, hoping a concrete suspect and confirmation from Jessica that Owen could pull this off and had motive are enough to save his badge.

"I don't know. I didn't talk to Owen much. Nina did, though. Since they're the best man and the maid of honor, they have to do a lot of things together. She might know more. That's all I have. I swear."

I turn to Quentin. He has to let her go. She might have hated three people at that table, but she didn't confess and she was never alone in the kitchen.

I stand up, knowing Quentin won't want Cam and me here to witness his suspension. "Good luck," I whisper to him as I pass.

Cam drives me back to the bed and breakfast. "Are you still going to try to figure this out if Quentin isn't on the case anymore?"

Quentin's not the reason I started looking into this case in the first place, and I'm in too deep to back out now. "I have an idea. We need to talk to Xander."

"Okay." Cam squeezes my leg.

The atmosphere at the bed and breakfast is chaotic at best. We find Xander in the library with Nina.

"We'll figure this out. I can't believe Jess would do something like this, but they're saying she confessed," Nina says.

"The only time she was in the kitchen with those drinks, you girls were with her. If none of you saw her touch the drinks, then there's no way she did." Xander puts his head in his hands.

"Maybe she's covering for someone," Nina says.

"Who? And why are people talking about Jess and Don? That's absurd."

"I don't know. She never mentioned anything to me, and she tells me everything."

I step into the library. "Sorry to intrude, but we'd like to speak to you both." Jessica suggested we talk to Nina to see if Owen said anything to her, so it's fortunate that we found Nina and Xander together.

"Jess told you everything, right?" Xander asks me. "You have to tell me what she said. The rumors going around this place are unbelievable. I need to know the truth."

"Xander, if I told you the truth is going to upset you, maybe almost as much as your friends dying, would you still want to know it?" I'm not sure how much he can handle right now. He seems like the sensitive type.

The color drains from his face. "Did she really do it? Did she kill them?"

"I don't think so. She didn't confess. That was a misunderstanding."

He lets out a deep breath. "What is it then?"

I swallow hard before continuing. "Xander, the police found Jessica's class ring in Donovan's pocket. Jessica confirmed that she and Donovan have been having an affair for the past four months."

Xander stands up, and signs of the broken soul I saw moments before is gone. He's furious. "How could he do that to me? He was supposed to be one of my best friends. If he weren't already dead, I'd kill him myself!"

At least this time, Quentin isn't here to mistake that for a confession.

Nina grabs Xander's arm and pulls him down to the chair again. "I can't believe this. You think you know a person, and then..." She shakes her head. "I'm going to get you a cup of tea or something. Stay here." Nina rushes out of the library.

"Xander, I know this is a huge shock to you, but we need to know if there's any chance Owen might have collaborated with Jessica to poison those drinks."

"Owen? I don't know. But I apparently don't know Jess at all. I mean we were engaged, and she was running around with one of my groomsmen. I don't know who I'm angrier with, her or Donovan. Probably Don because I've known him longer."

"I understand. A few years ago, my boyfriend had an affair with my best friend. We weren't engaged but we'd been together for years."

"How do you deal with it?" he asks me.

"I ask myself that every day. You know the detective working this case?"

He nods.

"That's him."

Xander's eyes widen. "I thought you two were together." He motions between Cam and me.

"We are. Now. It all worked out for the best. I'm just

glad I didn't marry my ex. And one day you'll be glad for that, too."

"You must have wanted to kill them," Xander says.

"I wished ill upon them, yes. But I'd never kill anyone. They aren't worth the jail time."

Xander laughs. "Thanks. I needed that."

"No problem. Back to Owen. You know him best. Could he have found out about Jessica and Donovan and killed that table full of people?"

"I'm not sure I know any of these people at this point."

"I understand why you'd feel that way, but for now, just pretend everything you thought you knew about them is true. Could he have committed murder?"

He releases a breath. "I've known Owen all my life. If he thought he was protecting someone he cared about, he'd do just about anything."

"Then, Xander, we need your help finding him."

"I wish I could help you, but I have no idea where he is. I do know this, though. Jess isn't the type to get her hands dirty. She liked Drew hanging all over her because he did anything she wanted him to. For all I know, she was having an affair with Owen, too. She could have talked him into getting rid of the guys she'd already tossed aside."

Xander is turning on his fiancée and his friends rather quickly. It makes me wonder if there's any chance he knew about all this before he came here, and he set up the entire thing to stage the perfect murder and make himself look like a victim.

CHAPTER THIRTEEN

By Friday morning, word of Quentin's suspension is all over town. Mickey is seated at his usual table, telling everyone the story. I walk over and sling my dish towel over one shoulder. "Mickey, can I speak to you for a minute?"

"Uh-oh. Mickey's going to get in trouble. I know that look on Jo's face," Mrs. Marlow says, circling an index finger in my direction.

"Drink your coffee, Mrs. Marlow," I say with just enough reprimanding tone in my voice.

She salutes me and takes a sip.

I lead Mickey to the far end of the display case, away from listening ears. "Mickey, you know I'm not Quentin's biggest fan, but even I feel for him right now. His entire life is that badge. He messed up. I get that. But let's not make fun of him for losing everything that means something to him, okay?"

"You're too good, Jo. Too good. But okay, I'll listen. This is your coffee shop, after all."

"Thank you. And as a token of my appreciation, I'll send Jamar over with a muffin on the house."

Mickey smiles. "Too good." He pats my arm before returning to his table.

I go back to the register.

"Everything okay?" Jamar asks me.

"Yeah, it will be. Would you bring Mickey a banana chocolate chip muffin, please? It's on me."

"You yelled at him, and now you're giving him a treat?" he asks.

"It works with Midnight," I say.

Jamar laughs. "You got it, Boss."

Sam comes into the coffee shop an hour later, her head down. Maybe even she understands that people are talking about Quentin. "Jo?" Her voice is small. "I did what you said. I checked in with every wedding about the flowers. No one ordered black carnations. I'm sure it was for the Pyle-Scanlon wedding. I remember the call to change the color, but the bride said I was stupid. I just don't get it."

I remember Jessica's complaint about the flower color. "You mean someone called and changed the color of the flowers?"

"Yes."

"*Changed*, not ordered the wrong color?"

"Yes. I'm sure of it."

Someone is trying to sabotage this wedding. Maybe

that's what this is all about. But who? And why mess with the color of the flowers? That's so minor in comparison to dead bodies. Unless, the killer took a different tactic when the murders didn't end the engagement.

"Samantha, I don't think you messed up anything. I think someone else did. Someone who doesn't want that marriage to happen. And now that Jessica's affair is out in the open, this person is getting their wish. The wedding is never going to happen."

"Well, that's sad."

"Not really. The bride-to-be was having an affair. Why on earth would her fiancé still marry her?"

"Love," she says matter-of-factly.

"The bride was in love with someone else."

"She should marry him then."

"She can't because he's dead." Dead. Everyone Jessica had a relationship with is dead, except for Xander. Maybe this is all about her. Someone might be out to destroy her by taking away everyone she loves. Drew, Donovan, and now Xander. "Sam, where's Quentin?"

"Next door in Bouquets of Love. Why?"

"I need to talk to him." I remove my apron and toss it under the counter. "Cam," I call, sticking my head in the window of the kitchen.

He comes over and taps my nose. "What's up, buttercup?" His smile fades when he sees my serious expression.

"I think this whole thing might be about Jessica. As in

someone is trying to ruin her life. I'm going next door to talk to Quentin. Do you want to come?"

"Yes, but no. He'll open up more if I'm not there."

Cam is the absolute best for understanding that.

"Okay, I'll fill you in as soon as I'm finished." I lean across the window, and he meets me halfway for a kiss.

"You two are so cute," Samantha says.

"Thanks. Now let's go." I hurry out with her, trying to ignore the strange looks from my customers. I'm sure they'll ask me all about it later.

Samantha opens the door to Bouquets of Love, and I step inside. Quentin's head pops out from the back room.

"It's okay to come out," I say. "I actually have information for you."

"I'm no longer on the case, Jo." He sits down on a stool behind the counter.

"Yeah, well not technically being on a case never stopped me from getting involved in your investigations, so why are you letting it stop you now?"

"She's right," Samantha says. "You should listen to Jo."

"I could get my suspension time increased."

"Or you could solve this case and redeem yourself to the chief. Maybe he'll lift the suspension all together." I cross my arms. "Do you want the information or not?" I tap my foot, knowing it drives him crazy.

"Okay, stop tapping. Tell me what you've got."

"I think someone is getting rid of the people Jessica cares about. Think about it. She was the only one who cared about Drew. He doted on her. His parents confirmed he loved her and would do anything for her. Then there's Donovan. Someone must have found out about the affair and killed him, too."

"If that's really true, Xander's life is in danger," Quentin says.

"I don't think so. Xander knows about the affair now. He'll never go through with the wedding. He's furious with Jessica. So essentially, the killer took Xander away from her, too. All we need to do is find out who hates Jessica enough to want to ruin her life."

"It has to be the best man," Quentin says. "Everyone seemed to know about Drew's obsession and how Jessica loved his attention. But if Owen discovered Donovan and Jessica were having an affair behind his best friend's back, he could have decided he was going to stop this wedding from ever happening by destroying Jessica. He even could have framed her for the murder. She was in the kitchen. She was at the table where the people were poisoned right before the drinks were served, too."

"We need to find Owen."

"I agree, but how do we do that? I put out an APB, but the guy seems to have dropped off the face of the earth. Without my badge, there's not much I can do."

"Not true. I do plenty to get in your way. And without your badge, you can't arrest anyone, which means they might be more willing to talk to you."

"Are you suggesting we go back to the bed and breakfast?"

"No one's checked out. That's where all your suspects and crime scenes are, so that's where we need to be to solve this."

"Let's go search Owen's room. See if he left anything behind that would tell us something."

"I thought you already searched his room."

"I did." He clears his throat.

"Oh, you want to see if I spot anything you missed." I can't even hide my smirk.

"We go over crime scenes a second time when we need to. It's not unusual."

"Of course," I say, turning toward the door so he can't see I'm full-on smiling now.

"I'll drive," Quentin says, walking around the counter and kissing Samantha goodbye.

"Go ahead. Cam and I will drive separately."

He pauses in the doorway and glares at me.

"You knew I'd bring him. Don't act surprised."

"Meet you there," he says. At least he knows better than to argue with me on this.

I run into Cup of Jo, and when Mickey sees I'm alone, he yells, "Do you need an alibi? We're happy to provide it. Just tell us what to say."

"I appreciate the offer, Mickey, but I'm good." I knock on the kitchen door. "Time to go," I call to Cam. "Robin, Jamar, are you both okay to run the place without us?"

"We've got it," Jamar says.

"Is it always this exciting here? I feel like you're

constantly rushing off to solve crimes." Robin is smiling from ear to ear.

"Only on the boring days. Thanks, you guys."

Cam joins me, ready to go.

On the way, I fill him in on the theory Quentin and I are working off of.

"You know what doesn't make sense to me?" he says.

"What?"

"How did Owen leave without anyone noticing? I mean there's night staff at the bed and breakfast. Wouldn't someone have seen him slip out?"

"No one saw anyone slip poison into those five drinks."

"I suppose, but it would take longer to get out of the building with his stuff. He'd also have to start his car, which would make noise."

"Unless he didn't drive," I say.

Cam turns to me briefly before focusing on the road again. "How else would he have left?"

"I don't know, but I'm sure some of them carpooled. There aren't enough cars in the lot for everyone to have driven themselves or even just their dates."

"You think he called for a car? They usually beep when they get there."

"He might have walked somewhere and then called a car service." All this hypothesizing is driving me crazy. I need at least one concrete answer to work from. So far, I have zero. "Do you think any of our theories are correct?"

"There's a good chance. This case is lacking evidence, though. That makes it tough to crack."

Five dead bodies and no evidence of anything but an affair.

Elena Reede meets us at the door. "I can't take this anymore, Jo. Everyone is going completely stir-crazy. And I'm honestly afraid of what's going to happen when Jessica comes back. They've all turned on her."

"All of them?" I ask.

She nods. "Even her bridal party. They're all claiming she wasn't who they thought she was. It's a nightmare. I'm afraid they'll gang up on her when she comes back. I'm thinking of calling the police and telling them they need to hold her at the station for her own protection."

"Did Quentin get here yet?"

"No, why?"

He must have parked around back so no one sees his car. Even though I'm sure he took his own vehicle and not a patrol car, people in town could still identify it as being his. I'm positive he wants to lay low until the case is solved.

"Elena, Quentin was officially taken off the case, but he's working with me to solve it anyway. If you can avoid telling the police that, I'd appreciate it."

"Okay. Whatever it takes to solve this case as soon as possible."

"I promise we're doing everything we can."

"We need to see Owen's room," Cam says.

Elena nods and goes behind the desk to get the key.

Quentin comes walking up to us from the direction of the kitchen.

"Where did you come from?" I ask.

"I came in the back. One of the staff members let me in."

"Elena knows the situation and is on board. She's going to take us up to Owen's room."

"This way," she says. "And, Detective, if you could do anything to restore order, I'd appreciate it. I swear they're planning a lynching for Jessica's return."

Quentin sighs. "Ms. Reede, call the station. Tell them you think it's in Jessica Scanlon's best interest to remain in police custody for the time being. If you explain the situation to the chief, he'll help you out."

"I will. Thank you." She brings us to the room opposite Nina's, and Elena opens the door. "I'm going to make that call to the station now. Let me know if you need anything."

"Thanks, Elena," I say before she disappears back down the hall.

The room looks empty. The bed isn't made, but there's no suitcase or overnight bag.

"We gathered he took his belongings and left in the middle of the night," Quentin says, moving to the nightstand.

I go to the bathroom and peek inside. The vanity is empty except for a bar of soap in the dish next to the sink. I reach for the shower curtain and pull it aside. A razor and a bottle of shampoo are resting on the ledge. "Looks like he missed a few items when he was packing up."

"He was most likely in a hurry," Quentin says.

Cam peers into the shower. "Too bad. That's an expensive razor."

"Not as expensive as life in prison," Quentin says.

He has a point, but I see Cam's, too. "Why would Owen just up and leave so suddenly? Doing so basically pointed the finger at himself."

"Which means he's guilty," Quentin says.

I guess so. Still, it seems odd to me, but then again, this entire case seems odd to me. "If Owen really did this to help Xander see Jess for who she really is and to take away the people Jess cares about, wouldn't he stick around to see his plan come to fruition?"

"Maybe he was afraid of being caught," Quentin says. "He could have felt we were getting close after questioning him."

"But why not try to get away with it. Running is the same as confessing, basically."

"She's right," Cam says.

We continue to search the room, when someone calls, "Owen? Is that you?"

I recognize Nina's voice before she pokes her head into the room.

She puts a hand to her chest. "You three scared me. I thought Owen was back."

"Why would that scare you?" Quentin asks.

"Isn't he your top suspect? I mean he ran away." Her gaze falls on me. "I probably should have told you this sooner, but Owen came to me before the party and told me he didn't know what to say in his speech because he wasn't sure Xander and Jessica should get married."

"What reason did he give?" I ask her.

"He wouldn't tell me. He hinted it was partially because of Drew. He said there had to be a reason why Drew stuck around, like he thought Jess was leading him on, letting him think he had a chance with her. I told him that was crazy." She shakes her head. "But now, I'm not so sure. I mean she had an affair with Donovan. I just can't wrap my head around it. If Owen knew about that, too, I can see why he was acting so strange."

"How else was he acting strange?" Quentin asks.

"Well, I knew there was tension between him and the other groomsmen, so I just assumed all the looks he shot that table at the party were because of that. Now, I think it might have been about the affair. I think that was worse in his eyes than Joseph dating his ex or Chris and Adam resenting him for being named best man."

"What was Owen's temper like?" I ask.

"He had strong opinions, and he didn't hide them. He was fiercely loyal to Xander, though. I've never heard those two argue about anything."

"We were at the police station earlier with Jessica, and she told us to ask you about Owen because you two worked on a lot of wedding preparations together."

"That's true." Nina lowers her head. "I still can't

believe she lied to me. I told her everything. I had no secrets from her. But you know, when I looked at the photos I took of her opening the engagement gifts, I saw it on her face. Her expression when she read Donovan's card said it all. She actually loved him. How is that possible? How could she do that to Xander? And how could she have spent enough time with Donovan to fall in love with him and not even tell her best friend?" Her lip quivers. "I'm sorry. I need to be alone right now." She turns and rushes to her room.

"I hate cases like these," Quentin says. "Frenemies. They lie to each other constantly, so you can't believe a word any of them says."

"You don't think any of them are telling the truth?" I ask.

"Maybe, but if that supposed truth was told to them and it was a lie, we're getting lies believed to be truths."

"Wow, that's confusing," Cam says.

"Welcome to my world." Quentin huffs.

I'm about to leave when I spot something behind the dresser. Whatever it is appears to be made of glass. "What's that?" I ask, not wanting to touch anything that might turn out to be evidence.

Quentin leans down to inspect it. "It's a small vial." He reaches into his jacket pocket and pulls out a tissue, which he uses to retrieve the vial. "Jo, I think you might have found what the poison was stored in," he says, holding it up for me to see.

CHAPTER FOURTEEN

The killer could have had the vial in their pocket at the party and just tipped it into the drinks. It would have taken only seconds, which explains why they were able to do it without being seen.

"How didn't you see this when you checked this room earlier?" I ask.

"I checked behind the dresser. It must have been underneath it at the time. It could have rolled across the carpet when someone walked by." He stands up. "Either way, this is going to nail Owen Pierce. I'm sure we'll be able to pull prints from it. I just need to get a bag to put this in so I can take it to the station."

I can't imagine the chief will be happy when Quentin shows up with evidence after being taken off the case. "Quentin, tell the chief I found it and called you." Technically, that's true. I did find it.

"Thanks, Jo."

I nod.

Quentin rushes out with the vial, ready to restore his reputation at the police station.

"Is that it?" Cam asks. "Does this mean Owen is the killer and the case is solved? Once they find him, that is?"

"I guess so. He had motive and the murder weapon. Not to mention he took off to avoid being caught."

"It feels a little anticlimactic."

I loop my arm around his waist. "If you ask me, I'm glad it's over. I'm ready to get rid of these people." They might have grown up here, but I'm glad they've since moved away.

"I wonder if the police will release everyone immediately."

For Elena's sake, I hope so, but since someone here might know where Owen would go, it's possible the police will want to talk to everyone one last time before they leave. We don't say a word to anyone as we head back downstairs. I'm not sure if Quentin even stopped to fill Elena in on what we found.

"You should ask her for the ring back the second she returns," Chris says. He's at the bottom of the stairs with Xander.

"Believe me, I'm not marrying her. I'm not sure I want the ring, though."

"Why not? You could sell it. Get your money back. Jess doesn't deserve to keep it."

"I'm not saying she does. I just want to be done with all of this. Forget it ever happened."

They look up when Cam and I reach the landing.

"Hey, any word?" Chris asks us.

I hold up my hands. "Sorry, but I'm afraid I don't have anything to share right now. I know the police are still looking for Owen, though. Any idea where he might have gone?"

"Far, far away, I hope," Chris says. "You picked the wrong girl and the wrong best man."

Adam walks up to them and claps Xander on the right shoulder. "I don't know. If Owen did kill those people, he might have done you a huge favor. The murders outed Jess's affair. He saved you from marrying her. I'd say that's about the only thing Owen's ever done right."

"Actually, if he knew about the affair, the right way to handle it would have been to tell Xander," I say. "You're all adults. You should be able to resolve conflicts without resorting to murder."

Adam holds up his hands. "Sorry, Mom." He starts laughing, and Chris joins in.

Cam looks ready to resolve some conflict with his fist, but I pull him away.

"He's not worth it. None of them is. I'll be happy to be rid of them."

"You and me both. How about I take you to dinner tonight to celebrate?"

"Celebrate what?" April asks from behind us. I'm not

even sure where she came from. "Did the police solve the case?"

"Not yet," I say.

"Well, are they still thinking it's Owen?"

"I believe he's the prime suspect, yes." I feel like I should put them all in one room and explain the situation so I don't have to keep repeating myself, but I've learned putting them all in one room can result in murder.

"When is Jess being released?"

This question draws a crowd. Elena was right. They've all turned on Jess. Even her closest friends.

I hold up my hands. "Okay, I don't know why you guys think I have all the answers, but I don't. I don't know when Jessica is being released. I don't know where Owen is. And I have no idea why you people pretend to like one another when you're stabbing each other in the backs all the time. I can't help you." I start for the door, but Elena stops me.

"You're leaving?"

I pull her aside and whisper, "We found the vial the poison was stored in. It was in Owen's room."

"So it was him."

"We think so. Now the police just have to find him. The problem is no one saw him leave."

"I checked with my staff. No one heard or saw anyone leave. Mr. Pierce didn't have a car on file with us. I take note of everyone's vehicles—make, model, and license plate number. He didn't leave one with us. If I remember correctly, he came in an SUV with several other guests."

"Do you remember which guests?" I ask.

"Yeah, it was the maid of honor and the engaged couple. They all checked in together. That's why they have rooms right next to each other."

Right. Jessica and Xander are on the end, and Nina's and Owen's rooms are on either side.

"Thanks, Elena."

"What should I do with everyone?" Elena pulls me aside, and Cam follows. "This group is really starting to scare me."

"Is your mother okay?" I ask.

"I moved her to my aunt's house this morning. She has a live-in nurse. They picked her up and are keeping her there until this is all over."

I don't blame her. I wouldn't want to stay here with these people either. I can't imagine Elena is sleeping well at night, even with a locked door. "I'll keep you posted on anything we find out. Hopefully, we'll find Owen and get a confession out of him soon. Then everyone will be free to leave."

"Jo, do you really think he was working alone? I mean, how could he pull this off and get out of here without anyone knowing? He had to have planned all of this well in advance to pull that off. Or he had help." Worry lines crease her forehead.

"That's a question we're still trying to answer." My phone rings, cutting me off. Mo's face appears on the screen. "Hold on one second," I tell Elena before stepping into the library for some privacy. "Hey, Mo."

Cam closes the door behind us so no one can eavesdrop.

"Jo, is everything okay?"

"Why do you ask?"

"Well, I was just at Cup of Jo, and everyone is saying the bride-to-be is getting death threats."

"What?" How would anyone even hear that if Jessica is being held by the police? "Mo, who said that?"

"More like who didn't."

"But Jessica is currently in police custody for her own protection."

"Because of the death threats."

Oh, the rumor mill has struck again. "No, that's not why. It's because her friends here are blaming her for everything, and until the police arrest someone for the murders, they don't want Jessica near these people."

"So no one has actually threatened her life?" Mo asks.

"No. I doubt she even has her phone on her."

"Want me to go back to Cup of Jo and set the story straight?"

I don't know how much we should interfere with this case, but things are getting out of control. "Mo, I need two favors. First, I need you to call the BFPD. Ask for Chief Caswell. Tell him what's going on in town with the rumors." I look at Cam because I know he's not going to understand why I'm doing this, but I feel like I have to.

"Tell him Quentin usually keeps the peace and distills any rumors, but without him on the case, people are running around scared."

Cam cocks his head at me.

"Quentin knows this case better than anyone else. Taking him off it was a huge step backward. People are going to be in a panic about a killer being on the loose."

"Okay, I don't really want to do Quentin any favors, but I guess I see your point," Mo says. "What's the second favor?"

"See what you can dig up on Owen Pierce. What does he do for a living? Who are his closest friends? Where is he currently living? Anything you can find that might help us figure out where he ran to."

"Got it. That's more my speed."

"Great, but call the chief first. Please, Mo."

"Fine. Quentin owes me after this, though. If I ever get a ticket, he better get me out of it."

"I'll be sure to tell him that. Thanks, Mo." I hang up.

"Do you really think Quentin will be able to get those rumors under control?" Cam asks me.

"I don't know. Honestly, I think Mo has a better shot at shutting them down, but I do think we need Quentin on this case."

"Why? There are other police detectives, and they're just as qualified as Quentin is."

"That might be true, but Quentin has more motivation to solve the case. He wants his badge back. He wants to redeem himself to the chief. No one is going to work harder than he will right now to find the killer."

Cam sighs. "I suppose you're right. What do you want to do next? Do we go back to work until we hear from Mo or Quentin?"

I'm too amped up to work right now. I'm dying to know if the vial we found in Owen's room will contain traces of the arsenic used to poison the drinks. If it does, that along with Mo's phone call to the chief might be enough to get Quentin back on the case in an official capacity. I'm so jittery I feel like I just downed an entire pot of coffee.

Cam rubs both of my arms. "Hey, are you okay?"

"Yeah, I'm just really tired of people using my coffee to commit crimes."

"Why don't we go get something to eat? You could probably use a good meal."

"Okay." Food does sound good right now. I open the library door to find just about everyone gathered in the lobby, waiting to hear what I have to say.

"Was that the police on the phone?" Paige asks. "Can we finally get out of here?"

"No, it wasn't the police. It was my sister," I tell her.

"Well, what are the police doing? Why is this taking so long?" Paige is getting irate now, and her cheeks are bright red.

I decide it's best to lay this all out for these people. If they want to get out of here so badly, then one of them needs to give us something useful so we can locate Owen.

"Look, Owen Pierce is at the top of the list of suspects. If anyone has any information on where he might be, now is the time to come forward. Without information, the police won't find him and no one will be going anywhere."

Xander steps to the front of the group. "I thought I knew Jess and Owen. They were the two people I was closest to, yet they both lied to me. I should know where Owen is. He should have confided in me because I'm his best friend, but apparently that was a lie, too."

Nina places a hand on Xander's shoulder. "They lied to all of us."

Xander puts his hand on top of Nina's and nods. Then he turns to the group. "When was the last time anyone saw Owen?"

"I saw him go to his room Tuesday night around eleven," Chris says.

"Did anyone hear any noises in the hallway Tuesday night?" Xander asks, his eyes going to Nina, presumably since her room was directly across from Owen's.

Nina bites her lower lip before saying, "I sleep with a white noise machine. I didn't hear anything in the hallway."

"What about you?" Paige asks Xander. "Your room is right next to his. If anyone would hear him, it would be you."

"I took a sleeping pill Tuesday night," Xander says. "It was the only way I was going to get any rest."

"Just wonderful," Paige says. "So we're all stuck here

with no clean clothing, and I'm running out of moisturizer."

"I'll have my staff restock the rooms with fresh towels and toiletries," Elena says, returning to her desk.

"Is there any way we can do some laundry?" Nina asks. "We're all running out of clothing. No one planned to be here this long."

"Yes, I really need my laundry done," Paige says.

Elena bobs her head. "If you gather your laundry by your doors, I'll have Grace come around to collect and wash it for you."

"Thank goodness," Laura says. "I thought I was going to have to turn my underwear inside out tomorrow."

"Do you need some help with the laundry?" Nina asks. "I'm guessing there will be a lot."

"Actually, if you all wouldn't mind bringing it downstairs to the laundry room, that would be a big help to my staff." Elena points down the hallway. "If you go through the kitchen, there's a door that leads to the basement.

There's a door from the kitchen to the basement? How didn't I know about that? That means that someone could have hidden in the basement and snuck into the kitchen when it was empty. They could have poisoned the drinks and snuck back into the basement without anyone knowing they were ever in the kitchen.

Everyone starts to move, but I yell, "Wait!" I hold up

my hand to the group. "Who here knew there was a basement?"

Heads shake all around the room. I should have known no one would come forth even if they did because it makes them look guilty. Time to try a new tactic. "Okay, who remembers seeing Owen at the party before the second servings of cake were brought out?"

More head shaking. So he could have gotten to the basement. "Elena, is there another way to access the basement?" I ask.

"From outside. There's a door at the back of the building."

"Did anyone see Owen leave the building that night?" I ask.

Xander's eyes widen. "During the party, he asked me for the car keys. He said he left the engagement card in the SUV. I told him my room was open and the keys were on the dresser. I'm assuming he went out to get the card because it was in the pile with the others when all the gifts were collected."

"We all know Owen killed the others," Nina says. "As difficult as it is to believe. Can we please just go get our laundry done now? I, for one, don't want to talk about Owen anymore."

The rest of the group is in agreement, so they go to retrieve their laundry. Cam and I stay with Elena, who seems more rattled by the minute. Once everyone is back with big bags of clothing in their hands, Elena and Grace bring us down to the basement. I go as well since I want to retrace Owen's steps.

Grace opens all four washing machines lining the side wall, but when she gets to the last machine, she screams.

Cam and I exchange a brief look before rushing over to her. Grace is rooted to the spot, pointing to the floor between the fourth washing machine and the first dryer where Owen's lifeless body is slumped.

CHAPTER FIFTEEN

I grab my phone and dial Quentin. It rings and rings before going to his voice mail. "Quentin, we found Owen. He's dead in the basement of the B&B. Get over here as soon as you get this message." I end the call and bend down in front of the body.

"Jo, don't touch anything," Cam says. He's holding the group back so no one can see the body.

"Is it Owen?" Paige asks.

I turn to face the group, but I don't stand up. "Yes. He's dead."

"How?" Nina asks. "I thought he was the killer."

So did I. *Come on, Quentin. Check your phone already.*

"Does this mean one of us is the killer?" Chris asks.

"Elena, call the police," I say. "Ask for Detective Perry. If he's not available, ask for the chief."

She hurries back upstairs, and I get the feeling she's relieved to leave the group and the latest crime scene. I can't imagine the Reede B&B will stay open after all this.

"Has he been dead since he disappeared?" April asks.

"The coroner will be able to answer that question," I say. "There's no sign of how he died."

"Do you think it was poison?" Paige asks. "Like with the others?"

That would make sense, but there's no evidence.

"Who was the last to see him?" Chris asks. "I saw him walk to his room, but I mean before that. Who was he with?"

"Me," Xander says. "We were talking in the living room. There were plenty of others around, though."

"Did you drug him with your sleeping pills and then kill him?" Paige asks.

Xander's head jerks back like he was punched. "What? No! I'd never do that."

These people really know how to turn on each other in a heartbeat.

"Everyone needs to calm down." Cam's voice is full of authority, and the room immediately responds to him. "I understand you're all scared, but this isn't the way to solve anything. The police will be able to determine the cause of death once they get here and examine the body. Until then, everyone should take a few deep breaths."

"Take deep breaths in the same room as a corpse? No thank you." Paige wraps her arms around herself. "I don't want to breathe in the stench of death."

The body doesn't smell, though, which means he

couldn't have died Tuesday night when he went missing. I turn to Grace. "Have any of the employees been down here since Tuesday?"

She nods. "Yes, I have. There wasn't a body. I would have seen it."

I look around the basement for places where Owen might have been hiding out. I'm not sure he'd stick around, though, when he could easily leave through the basement door. But that would mean he came back, and why would he do that?

I tug on Cam's arm and pull him away from the group. "Owen left undetected, so what would make him come back?"

"Maybe he planned to kill someone else."

"Or my earlier assumption was correct, and he had an accomplice. Maybe he was coming back to work out a way to either clear his name or get his accomplice out without anyone seeing."

"We need to check his phone to see who he talked to," Cam says. "Think it's on him?"

"Probably, but I don't want to touch the body. I don't want my fingerprints on anything that belongs to Owen."

Cam nods. "If the chief sends someone other than Quentin, finding your fingerprints on Owen's phone would point the finger at you again."

The sound of sirens outside alerts us the police are here. The question is who did they send?

"I don't think I've ever wished for Quentin to show

up before," Cam says, lacing his fingers through mine as we watch the basement door.

"Same here," I say, giving his hand a squeeze.

A team of people come into the basement, including the chief, the coroner, the forensics team, and the same police officer Quentin worked with earlier. Finally, Quentin walks in after everyone else, and I release the breath I didn't realize I'd been holding.

Quentin's gaze finds Cam and me, and he gives us a small nod. The other police officer brings everyone upstairs for questioning. Everyone but Cam and me. Quentin waves us over to the chief.

"You found the body?" Chief Caswell asks.

"Actually, Grace did, but we were right there with her," I say. "It doesn't appear he's been dead for too long."

"No smell," Quentin says with a bob of his head. "He must have been hiding out, but why didn't he make a run for it? He had to know it was risky to stay so close after his disappearance."

"I agree. And the only explanation I can think of is that he was working with someone."

Chief Caswell holds up one hand. "All signs point to Owen Pierce being the killer. Maybe someone tried to stop him from escaping. It's possible one of the other party guests figured out what Owen did and took the law into their own hands."

My phone rings in my pocket, and I pull it out to see

it's Mo. "Would you excuse me for a moment?" I ask the chief.

He doesn't look happy for the interruption, but I take the call anyway. It's not like I'm on his payroll.

"What do you have for me?"

"First, you're welcome. I got the chief to agree to let Quentin back on the case."

"I know. He's here. Thanks."

"He's there already?" she asks.

"Well, considering we found Owen dead in the basement, he sort of has to be here."

"He's dead? But I thought he was the killer."

"He might still be. Or one of them, at least. What else do you have for me?"

"Owen works as a pharmaceutical salesman. He currently lives with Xander. They're roommates. Owen has some hefty debts, too. College loans for one. And then he got into some trouble gambling. From what I found, he has no living family members to help him out. The way I see it, he can't afford to not have a roommate, so Xander marrying Jessica and moving out posed a problem for Owen."

But is that a big enough reason to try to stop a wedding? Not alone. Couple it with his anger toward Haley and Joseph, and maybe we have something. And being a pharmaceutical salesman, he probably knows a lot about drugs. Drugs!

I whip around to the chief and Quentin. "Owen is a pharmaceutical salesman, and Xander said he took sleeping pills the night Owen went missing. I'm willing to bet Owen was the one to not only provide the sleeping pills but suggest Xander take them. He had to make sure Xander wouldn't hear him in the next room when he made his escape."

"Whoa," Mo says. "I guess I found a missing piece to your puzzle."

"You did. Thank you. I've got to go."

"Good luck," Mo says before ending the call.

"We'll follow up with Xander to be sure, but that theory sounds plausible," Chief Caswell says.

"Chief," the coroner says. "I can't say for sure yet, but this looks to be another poisoning. If I had to guess, I'd say he's been dead for about twelve hours."

"Why would he come back?" Quentin asks. "There's no way he's been hiding out here this whole time. He must have left."

"Chief," a member of the forensics team calls. "You're going to want to see this." He places a piece of paper in an evidence bag and brings it to us. "Looks like we have a suicide note."

The chief reads it aloud. "'I couldn't take it anymore. Being betrayed by my closest friends and not having them blink an eye over it was too much. I poisoned their drinks Saturday night. I didn't think it was enough to kill them. I just wanted to make them pay for hurting me. After they died, I thought the police would figure it out, so I ran. But I couldn't live with the guilt. It only seemed fitting to end my life in the same way. Tell my family I'm sorry.'"

Something about the letter bothers me. He planned all of this ahead of time. Who goes through all that trouble if he only meant to make those people sick?

"Well, I guess that's that," Chief Caswell says. "We've got a confession. Case closed."

"That's it?" I ask. "What about our theory that he wasn't working alone?"

The chief holds up the letter. "This says otherwise. He took the blame. He didn't mention having a partner."

"Besides, you said he was a pharmaceutical salesman. That means he had knowledge of a lot of drugs."

Apparently not enough if he really didn't mean to kill those people. Why isn't anyone else questioning that?

Quentin crosses his arms. "It all adds up, Jo. We have our killer."

"Let's get the body out of here," Chief Caswell says. "We'll get statements from the rest of the guests, and they'll be free to leave in the morning."

He's letting everyone go.

I shake my head at Cam, not happy with how neatly this all wrapped up. It can't be that easy.

"Quentin, are you really satisfied this is over? I mean, Owen had reason to want to harm Haley and Joseph, but what about the others?"

"It's like we thought earlier. It was too difficult to figure out which frappes those two would drink of the five, so he poisoned them all. Since he didn't mean to kill anyone, he probably didn't feel too badly about making the other three sick. After all, he knew Xander hated Drew, so Owen probably felt Drew deserved it. And maybe he did know about Donovan's affair with Jess. He might have been trying to punish them all."

"But shouldn't we find out?"

"How? The man is dead, Jo. How do you propose we ask him?"

"Check his phone records. See if he texted or called anyone else who might have been in on this with him."

Quentin's gaze flicks to the chief before returning to me. "I just got my badge back. I can't go stirring the pot so soon. You have to understand that and let this go, Jo."

Maybe he can't stir the pot, but I can. I walk away from him and start upstairs again. "Cam, we have until the morning to figure this out. After that, they're letting everyone go, and Owen's accomplice is going to get away with murder."

"You don't think this was a suicide, do you?"

"Not at all. Owen didn't seem like the type to give up. He ran away. I'm sure of it. Something brought him back here. Or rather some*one* did. We need to find out who."

"How? We can't exactly ask everyone to show us their phones. Besides, I'm sure they would have deleted any incriminating messages."

He's right. The presence of very little evidence in this case means the killers are good at covering their tracks. They wouldn't be stupid enough to leave text messages on their phones.

The police have everyone in the living room, and as soon as we get to the lobby, an officer ushers us to the front desk. "Chief Caswell asked me to personally see you two to your car."

He actually called up here to make sure we leave. Unbelievable. Being that this is a crime scene, I can't fight it either by saying I'm Elena's guest.

"Come on, Jo. We've done all we can." He takes my arm and leads me to his SUV.

"Cam, we can't just leave."

"We can't stay either." He opens the car door for me. Once I'm in, he closes it and gets in the driver's seat.

"So, what do we do?" I ask as he starts the engine.

"We pull an all-nighter to figure this out. Then we come here with concrete evidence first thing in the morning before anyone leaves."

Easier said than done. "How do you propose we get concrete evidence when we can't get near the crime scene?" I ask.

"I have no idea, but I have a feeling this is going to involve a lot of coffee."

CHAPTER SIXTEEN

Mo and Jamar are at my door when Cam and I arrive.
Mo holds up a bag of takeout food. "Chinese anyone?"

"Please," I say, opening the door to my apartment.
Chinese food usually goes best with black tea, but I need
some strong coffee right now, so I brew a pot.

Once Mo and Jamar are up to speed on the case and
dinner is mostly eaten, we start spouting out theories.

"What if Owen came back to help Jess?" Mo asks. "I
mean everyone turned on her. Maybe he found out about
that and came back to clear her name."

"That would negate our theory that he found out
about the affair and was angry with Jess for hurting his
best friend. We have no evidence that Jess and Owen
were close, so why would he stick up for her instead of
Xander?"

Mo slumps back in her chair. "You're right. That

doesn't make sense. Man, this stuff is hard. I'm much better at looking things up online."

"Then do that. Go on Owen's social media profiles. See who he talks to the most." As soon as I say it, I realize I'm wrong. "No. See who he is connected to online but doesn't actually talk to there."

"Why?" She furrows her brow at me as she reaches for a fortune cookie.

"Because I think these two are smart. They'd communicate without anyone else knowing."

"Like coded messages?" Cam asks before finishing his last bite of egg roll.

"Maybe."

"You know, from everything you've told me about this group of people," Jamar says, "I wouldn't be surprised if they're all in on it together."

"Over twenty people in on the same crime?" Mo says, shaking her head. "No way. When was the last time you found twenty people who could agree on something?"

"She has a point," Cam says. "These people barely get along. Most of them don't even like each other."

"Except for the bridal party," I say. "They seem to be as thick as thieves."

"That's true," Cam agrees. "And if they were in on this together, then it would have been all too easy to poison the drinks when they were in the kitchen getting the wine."

"But that would mean that Jess was in on it, too," I

say. "And she definitely didn't want to kill Donovan. She was broken up over his death."

"What if some of the bridesmaids distracted her while one of them poisoned the drinks?" Mo suggests, grabbing her coffee mug with both hands.

"That could have worked. But again, where's the proof?" I don't envy the police for needing evidence. Usually, I don't worry about the evidence. I just point Quentin in the direction of the killer and let him prove it. This time, I can't. He's set on letting everyone go and pinning everything on Owen, which is exactly what Owen's accomplice wants.

"Do any of you think Owen was actually innocent?" Jamar asks.

"No," we all say in unison.

Jamar laughs and holds up his hands. "Okay, okay. I get it. Running sort of did admit guilt."

"I think the vial in Owen's room suggests he supplied the poison. I also think he used the excuse of needing to go get the card from the car as his means to leave the party, sneak into the basement from the outside, and put the poison in the kitchen through the basement access. It kept him out of sight so no one could pin this on him." I get up and start clearing the table.

"But then why run? He was careful enough to make sure he wasn't spotted." Mo dumps her empty container in the garbage can and leans on the counter to face me.

"I think he panicked when we started questioning

155

him. He slipped up and admitted to following Haley into the kitchen."

"He probably figured there was a chance someone saw him do that, so he had to come clean about it," Cam says, placing his coffee mug in the sink.

"Right, and going into the kitchen with Haley wasn't part of the plan. He just reacted in the moment because he was angry. Owen is very reactionary. He probably ran without thinking about the consequences."

We move to the living room and sit down. I bring my coffee mug with me and cuddle up on the couch next to Cam. "He took the time to plot the murders—"

"Wait," Cam says, angling his head down to see my face. "You think the part of the note that mentioned it being an accident was a lie?"

"I'm not sure. Given his line of work, you'd think he'd have knowledge of poisons and what doses would be lethal. But whether he intended to kill them or just make them sick, he planned it out. And then he ruined that plan in an instant when he got upset with Haley."

"Exactly," Mo says. "Clearly the guy is terrible at sticking to a plan."

"Doesn't that make a strong case for him not working alone?" I ask.

"It does," Cam says. "If someone else plotted this, and Owen's part was merely to get the poison and put it in the kitchen without anyone seeing, who is the real mastermind?"

"Why isn't anyone looking at Xander?" Jamar says. "He was Owen's best friend."

"That's true, and normally I'd say it makes perfect sense that Xander could have discovered the affair and plotted this with Owen, but then why would Owen need to give Xander a sleeping pill?"

"Who says he really did?" Jamar asks.

"Okay, but if Xander lied about that, then how do you explain his reaction when he learned about the affair. It seemed genuine to me."

My mind goes back to the night of the engagement party. The look in Xander's eyes when he stared at Jess was real. "No," I say. "He loved her. You can't fake the way he was staring at her like she was his entire world."

"There's a thin line between love and hate," Jamar says. "I think you know that's true, Jo."

"You think Owen planned this and brought Xander on board the night of the party?" I shake my head. "They'd never pull it off that quickly, and besides, Xander wasn't near the kitchen or the table that was served the poisoned frappes. It can't be him."

Mo slumps back on the couch and rests her head on a throw pillow. "We're getting nowhere."

I look at the time on my phone. We've been at this for hours and still can't prove a thing. "Jamar, you need to get some sleep. Cam and I are going to need you to cover Cup of Jo in the morning."

"You want me to open the shop?" He looks terrified

by the idea. "I mean I can turn on the coffee machines just fine, but I'm no baker."

"I'll go in early and make sure everything is baked and in the display cases before you start the day," Cam says.

"Then you should go, too." I pat his thigh.

"No way. We said we were pulling an all-nighter to figure this out."

"I know, but we can't let our business suffer to solve this case."

"She's right. It's not your job," Mo says. "And speaking of jobs, I have one to get to early in the morning as well. I'm heading home."

I stand up and walk her to the door. "Thanks for coming over. I'm sure you would have rather spent the evening with Wes."

"To be honest, he was weird at work today."

"How so?" I open the door and lean my head on it.

"I asked him if he wanted to grab lunch, and he said he had too much work to do to take a break. I asked if he could do dinner instead, and he said he'd let me know at the end of the day, but when I went to leave for the day, he was already gone. He didn't even say goodbye." Her shoulders droop, and she looks down at the floor. "I think maybe you were right, and we moved too quickly."

"I'm sorry. What are you going to do?" I ask, placing my hand on her forearm.

"Lay low, I guess. I wasn't looking for anything serious when I met him, so…whatever. I'll be fine." She raises her gaze to meet mine. "If he comes into Cup of Jo, don't go poisoning his coffee or anything, okay?"

"I've never poisoned anyone, and I'm not about to start." Although, I am tempted to slip a laxative into his coffee so he has to spend his day in the bathroom and deal with the humility of everyone he works with knowing he has diarrhea. My big sister claws are out.

"Good luck figuring out the case, but if you can't, don't lose too much sleep over it. Quentin might be right. This might be exactly what it looks like: a guy who accidentally murdered five people he just meant to teach a lesson and he couldn't deal with it."

I nod. "Goodnight, Mo."

She gives me a small wave and leaves.

"Will I see you in the morning?" Jamar asks.

"Probably, but if not, Cam will let you into Cup of Jo."

Jamar squeezes my elbow. "You can't win them all, Jo." He walks out and right into his apartment, shutting the door for the night.

"Are you sure you don't want me to stay?" Cam asks, his jacket draped over one arm.

"Want you to? Yes, but we should both get some sleep."

He leans down to kiss me goodnight. "Don't be so hard on yourself. If someone does go free, it's not on your head. It's on Quentin's and Chief Caswell's."

"I know. See you in the morning."

Just as Cam steps out, Midnight comes walking into

my apartment. I bend down and scoop her into my arms. "Hungry?"

She meows.

"I know. Silly question. I'm closing my door for the night, so if you're staying, you're stuck until morning."

She meows again.

"Don't say I didn't warn you." I get her some food, take a quick shower, and head to bed, where Midnight is already curled up on my second pillow.

I wake up at four in the morning with one thought in my head. I bolt upright in bed, disturbing Midnight, who meows in protest. "Owen didn't commit suicide, and I can prove it!"

CHAPTER SEVENTEEN

I race to Cup of Jo, knowing Cam will already be there getting all the baked goods ready for the day. "Cam!" I yell, running to the kitchen.

He drops a tray of scones, which clatters to the ground. "Jo, what's wrong?"

"I'm sorry! I'm fine. I didn't mean to startle you. It's just that I realized something, and it proves Owen didn't kill himself."

Cam grabs the tray and dumps the scones into the garbage. "How can you be so sure?"

"Remember what Mo found out about Owen?"

He starts making a new batch of scones. "Refresh my memory."

"He had a lot of debt, and he needed Xander as his roommate because he didn't have any family to help him out."

"So?"

"So, don't you remember what the suicide note said?" I make air quotes when I call it a suicide note, since I now know that's not what it was.

Cam shakes his head.

"It said to tell his family he's sorry. He doesn't have any living relatives. That proves he didn't write the note. And whoever did didn't know his family was dead."

"Then he was murdered."

"By his accomplice. I'm sure of it. We have to tell Quentin and the chief so they don't release the people from the B&B."

Cam looks down at the scones he's making. "Go. I'll finish up here and get Jamar set for the day. I'll call you when I'm finished, and we'll meet up wherever you are."

I rush over and kiss him. "I'll keep you updated."

He smiles. "I should have known you'd figure this out in time. Good job, Jo."

I return the smile and rush out. I call Quentin on the way to the station. His groggy voice tells me I woke him up.

"Quentin, it's Jo. You can't let anyone leave the B&B. I can prove Owen didn't commit suicide. Someone at the B&B killed him to keep him quiet."

"What time is it?" he asks.

"Four thirty-four, but that doesn't matter. I have proof Owen didn't write the letter." I tell him what Mo discovered about Owen.

"Okay, but what if he meant his friends when he said family? A lot of people without living relatives consider close friends to be their family since they don't have anyone else."

"Seriously? That's what you're going with? Do you understand there could be a killer at the B&B, and you're about to set them free?"

"Where are you now? And don't say on your way to the B&B."

I'm not. I'm on my way to the station, but maybe that's a better idea.

"Jo, listen to me. I'm supposed to be there at eight o'clock when the guests are released. Do not go to the B&B. Meet me at the station. I'll leave now."

"But—"

"Do you want my help or not?"

"Fine. I'll meet you at the station." I'm thinking I should talk to Jessica anyway. I hang up, which I'm sure sends Quentin into a panic since he doesn't trust me. It's ironic really since he's the one who broke my trust years ago.

The police station is pretty deserted at this hour. The chief isn't in yet, and I beat Quentin, so I take a seat at Quentin's desk and wait. He arrives about twenty minutes later.

"Took you long enough," I say.

"I did a little research of my own to confirm what you told me. It doesn't seem like Owen Pierce does have any living relatives, so you could be on to something. The problem is we have no evidence that points to who might have killed him."

No evidence. I'm getting really tired of those two words in connection to this case. The only evidence we found was the vial the poison was in. Wait. "Quentin, you searched Owen's room and didn't find the vial. What if that's because it wasn't in Owen's room when you searched?"

"You mean someone else planted it there later," he says, following my line of thinking.

"If I'm right, and Owen brought the vial to the kitchen so someone else could use it to poison the drinks, then he wouldn't have had the empty vial."

"Or you're wrong and he poisoned the drinks on his own."

"Can you entertain the notion that I might be right for a minute and try to figure it out?" Why else would he agree to meet me here if he isn't willing to do that?

"Okay, let's say you're right and he was working with someone, it would have to be someone in the bridal party or Jessica."

"Yeah. I think we should talk to Jessica. Maybe she can tell us more about what happened in the kitchen when they took the wine."

"Alright. Let's talk to her. She's downstairs in a holding cell." He motions for me to follow him.

"How did you get her to agree to stay in a holding cell?" I ask.

"When she heard that everyone at the B&B had turned on her, she didn't want to leave. She didn't put up a fight at all. I think she was terrified the killer would come after her next."

"Have you talked to her?"

"Not much."

"Did anyone tell her about Owen?" I ask.

"Yeah, the chief did last night. He said she wasn't exactly relieved she could leave today. I think she's worried about the repercussions of her affair now that all her friends know about it. My guess is she'll pack up her things in a hurry and get far away from Xander and everyone else she knows. Start over somewhere new."

And probably not change her behavior at all. It amazes me how often people don't learn from their mistakes.

Jessica is sleeping on the cot in her cell when Quentin unlocks the door. She stirs at the sound. "Is it morning already?"

"Very early morning," I say. "Jessica, we're sorry to wake you, but we need to talk to you about Owen."

"What about him?"

"Did he know about your affair with Donovan?"

"I don't think so." She sits up and swings her legs off the bed.

"What about your bridal party? Is there any chance one or more of them knew about it?" I ask.

She shakes her head. "I didn't even tell Nina, and I tell her everything. She's the only one who knew why I kept talking to Drew."

"Which was?" Quentin asks.

She runs her fingers through her hair. "Have you ever had anyone look at you like you're the most important person on the planet?"

I have. Cam looks at me that way.

"You're smiling," Jessica says, "so I know you understand what I'm talking about."

Quentin turns to me.

"It's the way you look at Sam," I tell him. "And the way Cam looks at me."

"You've looked at him that way for years." Quentin clears his throat, and for the first time I understand that my relationship with Cam couldn't have been easy for Quentin to deal with. It doesn't excuse what he did, but I do feel bad if Quentin felt like he came second to Cam when we were dating.

"I didn't realize," I say.

"I know." He turns back to Jessica. "Someone must have known about the affair, and that person helped Owen Pierce kill your friends."

"We think it has to be one of your bridesmaids. You were all in the kitchen when you stole the wine. We figured out that Owen left the party under the pretense of going to the car. Then he reentered the B&B through the basement door in the laundry room. There's a staircase that leads directly to the kitchen. He used it to place the vial of poison somewhere in the kitchen."

"I didn't see it when we took the wine."

"I didn't think you would have. He wouldn't have left it in plain sight."

"Were you the one who grabbed the wine?" Quentin asks.

"Yes. I took it from the wine rack."

"Then you turned your back on the bridal party," I say. "Any one of them could have grabbed the vial during that time."

"I didn't turn my back on all of them. Laura was in the doorway, standing guard. I saw her the entire time."

That leaves, April, Nina, Justine, and Paige. "How long would you say you were in the kitchen?"

"Two minutes tops."

The wine rack is next to the counter where I had my coffee machines and blenders set up. All this woman had to do was take a few steps back and slip the poison into the drinks. The vial had to have been hidden right next to the drinks.

"Jessica, I need you to think. Did anything happen in the kitchen? Did anyone stumble or spill anything?"

"No, nothing like that. I grabbed the wine from the rack, and we left."

"Who is the least trustworthy among your bridal party?" Quentin asks.

Jessica lowers her head. "I suppose I shouldn't feel so bad about throwing anyone under the bus when they're all probably talking about me behind my back now."

"Clearly, you're aware of how your friends act. They're quick to turn on each other. I mean Owen turned on Donovan and Joseph."

Jessica sniffles. "Did Xander turn on me?"

"What do you think? You cheated on him," Quentin says, completely shocking me. Maybe he does finally understand what he did wrong.

She starts sobbing. "I never meant for any of this to happen."

"Jessica, whether you did or not, this *is* happening, and we need your help."

"I don't know. I haven't been friends with Paige as long as the others. She's got a temper. Maybe she helped Owen. I know she thought he was cute."

I've seen how snippy Paige can be. The problem is, I don't think Paige is the type to confess. She'd go down swinging, which means we need her to slip up and implicate herself. I can only think of one way to get her to do that.

"Jessica, we're going to need your help if we want Paige, or whoever did this, to confess."

"My help? What can I do? I'm stuck in here." She holds out her arms to indicate the cell.

I turn to Quentin. "I want to take her with us to the B&B."

"Are you crazy? I'm not planning to bring her back there until everyone else is gone."

"Then we'll never catch the killer. Look, Owen might have had a hand in plotting this, and he definitely provided the poison, but someone else went through with the plan and later killed Owen. That person is in the B&B right now. If we want to draw them out, we need to find out who is angry enough with Jessica that they'd commit murder."

"You want to allow this person to try to kill me?" Jessica shrieks.

"No. I want you to make this person so angry that they slip up and confess."

"How? All killing Don and the others did was break up the wedding. Xander will never marry me now."

That's it! That's what this was all about. Breaking up the wedding. Maybe not the part Owen played. I think he really did want to hurt Joseph and Haley. But the second person did this to break up the wedding. And she has to be the same person who called Samantha to change the flower color for the wedding.

"Jessica, which of your bridesmaids has a thing for Xander?"

"None of them. That's insane!"

Quentin looks to me. "Maybe it's not."

I can't believe he's backing me up on this.

He turns back to Jessica. "Did Xander know any of them before you?"

She shakes her head. "No. They were all my friends."

"Even Paige?" I ask.

"Well, yeah, but now that you mention it, she was upset the night Xander and I got engaged. When I asked her what was wrong, she said she'd never find a man like Xander."

Like Xander or did she actually want Xander for

herself? "Jessica, will you please come with us and try to get Paige to confess?"

She bobs one shoulder. "It will never work. Xander isn't going to marry me, so why would Paige confess to anything?"

I reach for Quentin's arm. "What if we get Xander on board with this plan? We can ask him to play along."

"He won't do it. Xander's too honest a person," Jessica says.

"You need to persuade him," I tell Quentin. "He might agree to it if it's the only way to draw out the killer."

Quentin looks at Jessica. "I'll pull Xander aside as soon as we get there and explain the situation. But you're going to have to play along."

"Are you in?" I ask her.

"This all happened because of me. I guess I have no choice but to be the bait."

That might be the smartest, most honest thing I've heard her say.

"Let's go catch a killer," I say.

CHAPTER EIGHTEEN

The chief isn't in yet, which means Quentin doesn't have to clear this with him first. Or maybe he does, but he's choosing to ignore that protocol. Quentin drives Jessica in his patrol car, and I follow, calling Cam along the way to fill him in and tell him to meet us at the B&B. Jamar showed up early this morning since he knew Cam and I would need to get a jump on solving the case. I'm really lucky to have such a good friend and employee. I might not have a ton of friends, but at least I know the ones I have are genuine, not like the group at the bed and breakfast.

Quentin takes Jessica into the library before any of the guests can see her. Then he asks Elena to get Xander and send him down. We have to talk to him and get the plan in motion before the others wake up.

When Xander walks into the library, he stops short at

the sight of Jessica. I quickly shut the door behind him so no one can overhear us.

"Xander, I'm so sorry," Jessica says.

"Don't. I don't want to hear it." He looks at Quentin and me. "Why am I here? I don't want anything to do with her."

"We know, but we need you to pretend to want to be with Jessica long enough for us to catch Owen's accomplice."

"His accomplice? I heard there was a suicide note."

Everyone had been cleared from the laundry room before the note was discovered. "There was, and do you know what it said?" When he shakes his head, I continue. "Tell his family he's sorry."

Xander's eyes narrow. "He doesn't have any family."

"I know. That's how we discovered this wasn't a suicide at all. He was murdered by the person he arranged all this with in the first place."

"You're telling me another one of my friends is behind all this?" His face pales, and I'm worried he's going to be sick.

"Actually, this time it's one of Jessica's friends. We think it's someone in the bridal party."

"Probably Paige," Jessica says. "She wasn't happy when we got engaged, so it's possible she was deliberately trying to stop the wedding."

Xander scoffs. "You did that all on your own. Were you ever going to tell me? Or were you just going to marry me and keep on seeing Don on the side?"

Jessica starts sobbing. "I know it was awful, but, Xander, we didn't mean for it to happen. Neither one of us wanted to hurt you. I loved you both."

Xander holds up a hand. "I don't want to hear how it happened or what you two had."

"Xander," I say, "if you really want this to end so you can move past it, we need you to pretend to forgive Jessica and tell everyone the wedding is back on."

He lowers his head. "I don't know if I can do that. I mean, even if I can bring myself to say those words, I'll never sound believable."

"You can say as little as possible," Quentin says. "Stick as close to the truth as you can. Mention how this is a difficult time and you need to hold on to those you love. You don't actually have to mention Jessica by name. We can have her tell everyone you're still getting married."

"As long as you're standing with me, they'll believe you, Xander," Jessica says.

"And when they ask me how can I still love her, what do I say then?" he asks, tears filling his eyes.

I move toward him. "You wouldn't be this hurt right now if you didn't still love her," I whisper to him. "That's the hardest part. But it will fade with time, taking the hurt with it." My eyes flit to Cam. "And when you find someone who really is worthy of your love, you'll know."

Xander takes a deep breath. "Will you help me through this?"

"Of course. Just try to do your best acting because

the more convincing you are, the more likely this woman is to snap."

"When? When are we doing this?"

"As soon as everyone is up," Quentin says.

Xander turns to Jessica. "I hope I'm as good an actor as you are."

Jessica breaks out into a fresh fit of sobs.

By seven, we hear people stirring upstairs. I had a feeling everyone would be up early to pack so they could check out the second Quentin gives the okay. We move Xander and Jessica to the living room, where they sit on the couch.

"People should start coming downstairs any minute now," Quentin says. "You would sell this better if you were holding hands when they see you."

Jessica holds out her hand, but Xander doesn't take it.

"I know this is hard, but dragging it out will only make it worse," I tell him.

Footsteps on the stairs let us know it's game time. I stare at Xander, who finally takes Jessica's hand.

Chris and Adam arrive first.

"What the hell is going on?" Chris asks, his eyes glued to Xander's and Jess's hands.

"We'll explain everything once everyone is down here," Quentin says.

"No way. Someone better start talking now," Chris demands.

If I wasn't convinced Owen's accomplice was a woman, I'd suspect Chris right now from his reaction.

"What's all the yelling about?" Paige asks as she walks in with the rest of the bridal party in tow. "No way. Jessica?"

"Hi, Paige," Jessica says. "Miss me?"

"Miss your lying, cheating—"

"Okay, everyone calm down," Cam says.

But Jessica isn't calming down. She's not done egging on Paige. "I'm the liar, huh, Paige? What about you? You've wanted Xander from the start. Admit it. That's why you were so upset when we got engaged. I guess before that you assumed we'd break up, thought the relationship wouldn't go anywhere. But when he gave me that ring, you lost it. You thought you'd lost your shot with him, right?"

"What are you talking about?" Paige asks. "I never wanted Xander." She tips her head to the side and says, "No offense, Xander. You're just not my type."

"You liar!" Jessica continues. "You told me you'd never find a man like Xander."

"*Like* him. Meaning someone with a career and an actual future. Most guys our age don't have jobs and are living with their parents. You found a good one. I was happy for you, but I wanted the same for myself and didn't think I'd find it."

"Will someone explain how this is even happening?"

Chris says. "Xander, she was screwing around with Don behind your back. How can you be with her? She's a cheater. You can't possibly forgive her or think she won't do it again."

"It was a mistake," Jessica says. "Don and I never meant to hurt anyone. Xander knows that now."

"Oh, and since Don is dead, you're going to pretend it never happened. His death doesn't erase it, Xander." Chris is really losing it.

"No one said it erased it. All we're saying is we want to move past it," Jessica says.

"Would you shut up? Just stop talking. No one wants to hear a word you have to say." Chris moves toward Xander. "Say something, man. Tell us why you're being so stupid."

All eyes are on Xander, including mine. He has to sell this performance because so far, no one is confessing, and I'm no longer convinced it was Paige either.

Xander takes a deep breath. "You don't just stop loving someone," he says. "Even if they hurt you. I thought Don was one of my best friends, and he went behind my back."

"Yeah, and you were pissed!" Chris says. "You said so. You said you hated him and Jess."

"I was angry. I didn't know how to react at first. But when Jess got here this morning, we talked."

He's doing a great job of sticking to the truth but still sounding like he wants to marry Jessica. I really don't know how he's pulling this off so well.

"I realized my feelings were still there. I don't want the ring back. I want Jessica to keep it just as much now as the day I gave it to her."

A tear rolls down Jessica's cheek. "I love you, Xander."

"No!" Nina yells. "Xander, you can't marry her. You can't possibly still love her. She never loved you the way I do. I'm the one who's been there for you. It was my shoulder you cried on. Why can't you see it?"

Cam and I exchange a look. Neither one of us is standing near Nina. Quentin steps toward her, his hand on his hip, where his gun is holstered.

"Nina?" Jessica says. "It was you?"

"Don't you dare give me that look, Jess. You don't deserve him or me. We're too good for you."

She hasn't actually confessed to anything but loving Xander. We have to keep pushing her. "Did you convince Owen that Joseph didn't deserve Haley?" I ask.

Nina whips her head in my direction. "Owen was an idiot. But Jess." She focuses right back on her supposed best friend. "First Drew. You bragged about how much that guy loved you. You didn't care that Xander hated him. You didn't care that you were hurting him by stringing Drew along. No. All that mattered was your ego. Drew made you feel good about yourself."

Xander's hand is limp in Jessica's. He's barely holding on to the act anymore.

"You know how I figured out you were seeing Don on the side?" Nina scoffs. "You got in my car one day and smelled like Don's cologne. I guess you forgot to shower afterward, huh? I started watching you and Don after that. I saw the way you two would act pleasant enough but keep your distance, like you were scared of being too close because your true feelings would reveal themselves."

I have to get her to confess to more than knowing about the affair, and there's only one angle I can see to play. "You decided to help Xander, didn't you?" I say. "But you were afraid he wouldn't believe you if you went to him with the truth."

"Look at him. He's with her now after knowing the truth. He's too a good a person to help himself. I had to do something."

"And by something, you mean make Jessica and Donovan pay for hurting Xander."

"Did you help Owen poison Don for me?" Xander asks her.

I breathe a little easier now that Xander is helping the situation again.

"I couldn't stand by and let them carry on like that."

"Why not just poison Jess?" I ask.

"Poison is too good for her. I wanted her to feel the pain of losing Donovan, Drew, and Xander. Watching Xander wind up with me in the end would be a constant reminder of her betrayal. She'd have to live with knowing she was the reason Don and Drew were dead."

"That's why you killed them," I say, knowing Quentin

needs to hear her say it. He needs a confession since there's no evidence to tie the murders to Nina.

"Nina," Xander says in the sweetest tone possible. He drops Jess's hand and stands up. In three strides, he's in front of Nina. "Did you kill them for me?"

Nina actually smiles. "Yes. It was all for you, Xander."

Quentin grabs Nina and cuffs her.

Xander steps back, his expression now one of disgust. "You're worse than they are," he says.

"No! Xander, please!" Nina tries to pull away from Quentin, but he has a firm grip on her cuffed hands.

Quentin reads her rights and gets her into the patrol car. Everyone is released, and they don't waste a second calling for rides. It's odd how most of them opt to pay for transportation rather than travel together. This past week destroyed a lot of friendships.

Cam wraps an arm around my waist. "In case I haven't told you lately, I'm really thankful to have you."

"I love you, too," I say, giving him a kiss.

"Let's go to Cup of Jo. I'm sure Jamar and Robin could use a break."

CHAPTER NINETEEN

Cup of Jo is full to maximum capacity. Everyone wants to talk about the murders, and when Quentin shows up to fill me in on how things went with Nina at the station, the entire place goes quiet.

"What do you have for us, Detective?" Mickey asks.

"You know I'm not going to give you details, Mickey." Quentin walks up to the counter. "You have a minute?" he asks me.

"Let me get Cam from the kitchen. He's been baking since we got here."

"You've got quite the crowd here, so I can see why."

"If you want to earn back some points with these people, consider letting them hear what you have to say. They're going to find out anyway."

I don't think there's any way he'll listen, but Quentin walks over to the table next to Mickey's. "Do you mind if Jo, Cam, and I use this table? We need to discuss the case. I'll trust you all not to listen in, no matter how loudly we might be talking."

Cam steps out of the kitchen with flour on his cheek.

"Nice look," I say, using my thumb to wipe away the flour.

He smiles at me. "I'm dying in there. The oven's been going all day."

"Go sit with Quentin. I'll make some nice cold frappes for us."

It's odd to see Cam and Quentin sitting together, but it seems that I can't avoid working with Quentin, and I'd never exclude Cam. I guess this is my life now.

"Are you making frappes?" Mo asks, making me look over my shoulder at her.

Wes is standing next to her.

"Hi, you two. I am making frappes. Should I make two more?"

"Please," Wes says. "The sun is strong today." He gently takes Mo's arm. "I'll try to find us some seats."

"Thanks," she says with a smile.

"Spill," I tell her.

Mo walks behind the counter to join me so we can talk without everyone overhearing. "Turns out my boss really did overload him with work. He even sent him out on an errand, which is why he was gone before the end of the day. He was on his phone so much the battery died, and he didn't have his charger."

"So you worried over nothing."

"Basically, yes. He apologized profusely even though

it wasn't really his fault. And he's taking me out to dinner tonight. You and Cam want to come?"

"On your date?"

"I'm trying to slow things down a little to avoid future freak-outs."

"I see. Well, how about you see how lunch goes and then text me later if you really want company on your date tonight?"

"You're the best, Jo." She looks out over the customers. "Looks like Wes can't find seats."

"Sit with Cam and Quentin. Quentin is going to fill us in on the case once I finish with these frappes."

"He's going to talk about the case with everyone listening in?" she asks.

"I told him it would help get people to dislike him a little less." I wink and then turn on the blender.

She laughs and walks toward their table. It only takes me a few more minutes to finish the drinks and put them on a tray. Cam is at my side to take the tray before I can carry it to the table.

"Thank you," I say. "You're very handy to have around."

"I try."

We take our seats, and everyone grabs a glass.

"What do you have for us, Detective?" I ask before sipping my frappe.

"Nina owned up to everything. I guess since she realized she couldn't have Xander, she at least wanted credit for what she'd done."

"Psycho," Mo says.

"Yeah, it was her plan from the start. At first, she just wanted to break up the engagement and stop the wedding, but when Owen confided in her that Joseph and Haley had started dating behind his back, she decided to take things further. She convinced him they could poison the people who hurt them. Owen was under the impression it wouldn't kill them, just make them sick. He even told her how much to give them to make sure they didn't die."

"And, of course, she took matters into her own hands," I say.

"She lied and said it was an accident. I guess Owen believed her since the plan had never been to kill anyone."

"She used him," Cam says. "It's crazy how she turned out to be the biggest liar of them all. She even one-upped Jessica."

"I suppose murder does trump cheating," Mo says, "though, for the record, cheaters are still some of the lowest people on the planet."

I nudge her foot under the table. Quentin is trying to be a better person, and I'm doing my best to let him. She meets my gaze and bobs one shoulder before sipping her drink.

"Did Nina tell you where Owen hid the vial of poison?" I ask Quentin, steering the conversation back to the case. I don't know why I want to know so badly, but I do. Maybe I'm curious if I would have discovered it had

I gotten back to the kitchen sooner and beaten the bridal party in there.

"Yes, he left the vial under a napkin on the counter behind the blender. That's how Nina kept her fingerprints off it. She never touched the vial itself."

By my blender. Yeah, I would have found it. I might have even touched it, which would have been awful because my fingerprints would have been on it. I'm not sure I would have recognized it as poison, so I probably would have left it, assuming it belonged to one of the cooks.

"Why did she end up killing Owen, though?" Cam asks. "After he ran, she could have gotten away scot-free."

Quentin sips his drink before answering. "That was her plan. She actually talked him into running away. She told him the police were on to them. She implied she was going to run away as well. When Owen left and realized Nina stayed behind, he went back. Apparently, he snuck in through the basement and called her, telling her to meet him down there. Nina pulled one over on him again, pretending she wasn't able to sneak away as planned because she shared a room with April, and April got suspicious. Nina told Owen she'd get her things together and leave with him. Then she slipped upstairs to the kitchen and got him a drink."

"A drink with a lot of poison, I presume," I say.

"You got it. He was stupid enough to drink it. She waited until she heard him fall to the ground. Then she went back to get the bottle of water and write the suicide note."

"But she slipped up and mentioned a family Owen didn't have," I say.

"Exactly. She claims that was her only flaw in the entire plan." Quentin shakes his head.

"Man, I work some overtime, and I miss all the good stuff," Wes says.

"Wait. You got overtime?" Mo asks. "I was supposed to work overtime, but our stingy boss decided he didn't want to pay me."

"He said that?" Wes asks, not looking happy at all. "Mo, if I'd known, I never would have taken the overtime."

"It's not your fault."

"I'm going to talk to Mr. Kimball. What he did to you is not okay."

"I don't want you getting in trouble for me. Don't worry about it." Mo waves her hand in the air, but Wes takes it and holds it in his.

"I'm going to worry about it. I'm not going to sit back and let anyone hurt you."

Mo's gaze goes to mine before she looks at Wes. "You're pretty incredible."

I have a feeling they'll be having dinner alone tonight, which is totally fine by me. Wes is a great guy, and it's clear he cares a lot about Mo. Besides, if they're dining alone, it means I get to spend the evening alone with Cam. And that's something I'd never complain about.

"I should get back to the station. I have a lot of paperwork to fill out." Quentin stands up. "What do I owe you for the drink?"

"Actually," Robin says, walking over to the table, "your drink is on Mickey," she tells Quentin.

"See what happens when you throw people a bone, Detective." I smile at him.

Quentin actually looks a little choked up. He dips his head to me, and I know it's a thank you he's unable to say at the moment. He turns and goes to Mickey's table. "Mr. Baldwin, thank you for the drink."

"Good day, Detective," Mickey says.

I get up and walk over to Mickey. "You're a big softy, aren't you?"

"Eh, I owed him one. I know he sat by my table on purpose."

That he did. "Can I get you all another round?" I ask his table.

"I've got it, Jo," Robin says.

"Thanks, Robin."

"She's really turning out to be a great addition to Cup of Jo," Cam says.

"She is, but my favorite addition to Cup of Jo is definitely Cam's Kitchen." I lean up on my toes to kiss him.

"Where can I take you for dinner tonight?" he asks, wrapping his arms around me.

"Hmm, I don't know, but I think that's a mystery we can easily solve."

If you enjoyed the book, please consider leaving a review. And look for *Lattes and Lynching*, coming soon!

You can stay up-to-date on all of Kelly's releases by subscribing to her newsletter: http://bit.ly/2pvYT07

ALSO BY USA TODAY BESTSELLING AUTHOR KELLY HASHWAY

Cup of Jo Mystery Series

Coffee and Crime

Macchiatos and Murder

Cappuccinos and Corpses

Frappes and Fatalities

Piper Ashwell Psychic P.I. Series

A Sight For Psychic Eyes

A Vision A Day Keeps the Killer Away

Read Between the Crimes

Drastic Crimes Call for Drastic Insights

You Can't Judge a Crime by its Aura

Fortune Favors the Felon

Murder is a Premonition Best Served Cold

It's Beginning to Look a Lot Like Murder

Good Visions Make Good Cases (Novella collection)

A Jailbird in the Vision Is Worth Two In The Prison

I Spy With My Psychic Eye Someone Dead

A Vision in Time Saves Nine

Madison Kramer Mystery Series

Manuscripts and Murder

Sequels and Serial Killers

Fiction and Felonies

Paranormal Books:

Touch of Death

Stalked by Death

Face of Death

Unseen Evil

Evil Unleashed

Into the Fire

Out of the Ashes

Up in Flames

Dark Destiny

Fading Into the Shadows

The Day I Died

Replica

Writing as *USA Today* Bestselling Author Ashelyn Drake

The Time for Us

Second Chance Summer

It Was Always You (Love Chronicles #1)

I Belong With You (Love Chronicles #2)

Since I Found You (Love Chronicles #3)

Reignited

After Loving You (New Adult romance)

Campus Crush (New Adult romance)

Falling For You (Free prequel to *Perfect For You*)

Perfect For You (Young Adult contemporary romance)

Our Little Secret (Young Adult contemporary romance)

ACKNOWLEDGMENTS

With every book, I love my publishing team even more. Patricia Bradley, your feedback and edits are appreciated more than I can ever express. Ali Winters at Red Umbrella Graphic Designs, you make cover art look easy in addition to absolutely gorgeous. My ARC readers and VIP reader group, thank you for your excitement and for sharing this journey with me. And to my readers (that's you!), thank you for taking the time to read my books.

ABOUT THE AUTHOR

Kelly Hashway fully admits to being one of the most accident-prone people on the planet, but luckily, she gets to write about female sleuths who are much more coordinated than she is. Maybe it was growing up watching *Murder, She Wrote* that instilled a love of mystery, but she spends her days writing cozy mysteries. Kelly's also a sucker for first love, which is why she writes romance under the pen name Ashelyn Drake. When she's not writing, Kelly works as an editor and also as Mom, which she believes is a job title that deserves to be capitalized.

 facebook.com/KellyHashwayCozyMysteryAuthor

 twitter.com/kellyhashway

 instagram.com/khashway

 bookbub.com/authors/kelly-hashway

CPSIA information can be obtained
at www.ICGtesting.com
Printed in the USA
LVHW111010110321
680885LV00042B/708/J

9 781953 800077